"Miss Pierce, if I may be so [obscured] **as to mention what** [obscured] **an unple** [obscured]

St. John's vo [obscured]

"Oh, yes, sir, [obscured] f. "I am so very gra [obscured] ance you and Lady Fitzwarren [obscured] me the other day in the Park. I cannot think what I should have done if your party had not been there at that particular moment to come to my aid."

She saw the self-effacing expression at once cross his handsome visage. He bowed.

"At your service, ma'am. My aunt played the greater part in assisting you, I believe."

"Oh, no, sir. You were very kind, and I am exceedingly grateful to you for your understanding. And yet more grateful for your putting it about that you did not come upon me by accident. I have been saved quite a deal of unpleasantness due to your actions on that matter, as well."

Sir Pennworthy's expression altered as she spoke. His fine mouth thinned to a line and his eyes, it seemed to Alethea, grew darker still.

"Are you yet free of—of unpleasantness, Miss Pierce?" he asked, his hard gaze searching hers. Under that gaze, Alethea suddenly felt as if she could not breathe. . . .

BOOK YOUR PLACE ON OUR WEBSITE AND MAKE THE READING CONNECTION!

We've created a customized website just for our very special readers, where you can get the inside scoop on everything that's going on with Zebra, Pinnacle and Kensington books.

When you come online, you'll have the exciting opportunity to:

- View covers of upcoming books
- Read sample chapters
- Learn about our future publishing schedule (listed by publication month *and author*)
- Find out when your favorite authors will be visiting a city near you
- Search for and order backlist books from our online catalog
- Check out author bios and background information
- Send e-mail to your favorite authors
- Meet the Kensington staff online
- Join us in weekly chats with authors, readers and other guests
- Get writing guidelines
- AND MUCH MORE!

Visit our website at
http://www.zebrabooks.com

THE
MARRYING
MAN

Kathryn June

ZEBRA BOOKS
Kensington Publishing Corp.
http://www.zebrabooks.com

ZEBRA BOOKS are published by

Kensington Publishing Corp.
850 Third Avenue
New York, NY 10022

First Printing: February, 2001
10 9 8 7 6 5 4 3 2 1

Printed in the United States of America

Dum licet, et loris passim potes ire solutis,
  Elige cui dicas "tu mihi sola places."
Haec tibi non tenues veniet delapsa per auras;
  Quaerenda est oculis apta puella tuis.

While yet you are at liberty and can go at large with
    loosened rein,
  choose to whom you will say, "You alone please me."
She will not come floating down to you through the
    tenuous air,
  she must be sought, the girl whom your glance approves.

—Ovid, *The Art of Love* I

One

There was something tantalizingly familiar about her. He had seen her before, certainly. But where?

St. John Rutherford Pennworthy, eyes narrowed in frustrated concentration, felt the jab in his side as if it had been directed from miles away. Dragging his attention away from the girl across the church aisle, he turned with mild irritation to the man who stood next to him—a fellow he had known for a third of his life and who therefore merited such cavalier treatment. It mattered not that they were standing by the altar of London's St. George's Church during the wedding of their closest friend.

The Earl of Alverston was looking at him with something akin to the frustration St. John felt at the moment. He simply was not able to place the girl he was absolutely sure he had met before, or at least seen from a distance. Who in Town did he *not* know? He was no shabby, cap-wearing recluse, after all.

His fine, blond brows rose in haughty impatience at having been disturbed from his rumination.

"The *ring,*" the earl whispered to him from between slitted lips, casting his glance meaningfully to the other side of St. John toward the altar and the groom. St. John's brows rose a fraction of an inch higher and his hand went to his waistcoat pocket as he turned to face the altar again. As he pulled forth the gold and diamond band, he could not help but notice that everyone was looking quite intently at him. He smiled—his winning smile, he had long ago discovered, cleared up most troubles—and extended the ring to the groom standing not four feet away from him. The bride caught his gaze, shy and yet merry despite herself; then she and the others turned back to the priest and the ceremony continued.

It seemed they had been waiting for him. Bother. Where *had* his mind gone wandering?

Where, *indeed?*

Having discharged his one and only task, St. John again set his gaze on the young lady across from him, one of the bride's two maidenly attendants. She was lovely, slim but not too slim, no angles or sharpness about her. Her chestnut locks were arranged in an intricate braid wrapped artfully around the crown of her head, a few stray tendrils left to delicately caress the lace at the high-necked bodice of her pale green gown. Her gloved hands were clasped gently around a bouquet of late-winter roses. Yellow. Not at all her color, he thought as he brought his gaze up to her face.

She was looking at him. One brow raised, hazel eyes assessing. St. John lifted a hand to his mouth, coughed lightly, and looked to the altar.

Marriage.

Lady Cassandra and Lord Bramfield made a lovely pair: her flaxen delicacy, his stalwart, copper-headed solidity; demure and sweet, good-humored and steady. A lovely pair.

St. John nearly sighed aloud. Nearly. He did not, of course. Noted Corinthians were not known for their die-away airs. Best leave that to poets and maidens.

He clenched his jaw in a manly fashion.

It was time, St. John suddenly knew, watching but attending more to his own thoughts as the priest said the final blessing and the viscount Bramfield kissed his newly wedded viscountess on the lips and took her hand in his. It was time to get married. St. John had wanted it for as long as he could remember, he had fought that desire for all he was worth—which was not insubstantial—for at least a decade, but now was finally the time.

Taking a deep breath, chest extending a bit as he restrained the tears that trembled familiarly somewhere in the back of his throat, St. John watched the couple walk down the aisle arm-in-arm. Yes, today was as good a day as any, was it not? Weddings made everyone feel romantic, did they not?

He turned and glanced at the girl still standing across the aisle from him, and he felt something stir inside of him. There were tears in *her* eyes as she smiled at the retreating pair. She had a heart, then. It did not at that moment occur to Mr. St. John Pennworthy that she would not, as per course, be quite willing to share it with him.

* * *

"You are made of presumption, my boy, and for that alone I adore you!" Lady Mellicent Fitzwarren waved a scented puce lace kerchief before her, ticking St. John on the edge of his well-shaped jaw. He raised a hand to his chin as if to brush away a gnat and looked fondly at his maternal aunt.

"I am flattered, madam, that you should find something in me to admire." His tone was dry, as she liked it, as—unaccountably—nearly everyone he knew liked it. "But I should, nonetheless, like to speak to the young lady alone."

His eyes strayed, but only for the briefest of moments, across the room to the young lady in question. As a member of the wedding party, she knew many of the other guests, as did he. She was standing amidst a group of the bride's people, some of them known to him, mostly girls of the new viscountess's age, and Lady Fredericks, the bride's mother and a particular friend of his aunt.

He could have stepped over to congratulate Lady Fredericks on her daughter's nuptials, but he did not think he could manage to converse with the unknown girl alone that way. He needed his aunt to draw the lovely thing away in her customarily eccentric manner, and then he could speak with her privately, or at least without others near about. He did not think he could wait any longer. The lavish wedding breakfast spread on the tables held no interest for him, although the three hundred or so other guests present were consuming it with quite ferocious vigor. St. John could think only that he was somehow certain she was The One. He could almost *feel* it in his blood. Finally, The Day had come, The Very Moment, and the pure joy of relief made him impatient to get on with it.

His aunt reached out and tweaked his cheek affectionately, but not without glee. One did not usually, after all, tweak any part of a wealthy None-such in his thirtieth year. Unless invited to do so, naturally.

"I shall do it for you, dearest Nephew, despite the fact that it sits ill with me to arrange for you secret assignations with innocent maidens." Her full lips were pursed, her chins resting on her garishly garbed and ample bosom. A tall, sea green peacock feather tilted over one side of her turbaned head. She was the stare of fashion, of course: she was a countess.

"Not secret, Aunt: just private."

"Private? At a rout of this size? Ha! M'dear, you must have more feathers under that golden cap of yours than the *ton* gives you credit for!" She laughed at her own joke rather heartily. St. John smiled benignly. He always smiled benignly at such comments; it was the only honorable— not to mention considerate—way to respond. She was looking around her. "I shall signal you when I find the opportunity. It *is* such a shame dear Prinny could not be here today. He has tried to put a good face on this whole Regency business—" (St. John chuckled, despite himself) "—but I'm afraid he finds that the responsibilities are fagging him quite to death."

His aunt went on, but since it was not St. John's concern whether their newly designated Prince Regent was present or overburdened or what have you, he attended her barely at all. Instead, he sipped sparingly at the glass of champagne in his hand, felt the rumbling of his empty, admittedly nervous stomach, and tried not to look too often across the room at the girl he would, hopefully by the end of the hour, ask to be his bride.

"I beg your pardon, sir?"

He was certain he had spoken clearly. Had he not been rehearsing this speech for most of his life? But she was looking at him so queerly, her hazel eyes wider than he had imagined eyes could be. Quite marvelously wide.

"There *is* something of a roar to overcome, even here," he said sympathetically, and moved closer to her in the corridor to make himself heard. She stepped back, not taking her saucer-round eyes from him.

"I said I hope, Miss Pierce, that you will do me the honor of marrying me."

The words felt delicious to say out loud finally, or out loud to a real, live woman at last. He could not count on the stars in the night sky the number of times he had said them to a field or a horse or a curricle or a spaniel or a tree, for stars enough there were not.

The real, live woman looked, if possible, even more bewildered.

"Mr. Pennworthy, I do not believe I have rightly understood you. Although I can hear you just fine, thank you," Miss Alethea Pierce added hastily, putting up her hand between them, seeing that he was intending to move closer again, his mouth open to speak. "I hesitate to suggest that it seems to me as if you have just made a proposal of marriage. But since we have only now spoken for the first time, and our parents have no previous understanding, I am certain this cannot be the case. Have you, perchance, mistaken me for someone else?"

She had not been able to resist sneaking in that question, her astonishment having agitated her mischievous streak rather neatly. And St. John Pennworthy was a notorious object of such jibes—even she knew that. But the look in the gentleman's dark blue eyes struck her uncomfortably.

"Indeed not, madam. I wished to ask you, for sure." His voice was even and she could find no hint of anger or amusement or hurt in his expression. "My parents have nothing to say in the matter, although I understand that others are not so fortunate," he explained reasonably. "If yours are the concerned sort, I shall most willingly go to them to request their approval, but I had hoped you would be able to give me yours first." He smiled, the expression reaching his eyes causing Miss Pierce's to widen yet more, if possible—this time in profound appreciation. For a moment she was speechless.

Then she gathered her wits and clasped her hands in front of her. She could hear the wedding breakfast continuing noisily in the adjoining room, and could not help but think it remarkable that no one had come into the corridor since Lady Fitzwarren had led her out here—other than Mr. Pennworthy, that is. On the other hand, she was glad of the seclusion; she much preferred to be humiliated in private. She had become quite a dab hand at that in recent weeks, after all.

"Sir," she heard herself say more bracingly than she intended. She tempered her tone. "Sir, you do me a great honor if you be sincere. I cannot, however, believe that you are, given our indescribably brief acquaintance and the circumstances under which you have spoken. I shall, however, endeavor to disremember that you have made me the recipient of such a prank, and we can now shake hands and leave this place amicably, if you please. I should like to return to the party."

St. John stared at the young lady, words disintegrating on his tongue. Sincere? She doubted his sincerity? However could she doubt his *sincerity*? He had never been more sincere about anything in his life.

"I am sorry to have offended you, madam," he said, his throat tight and dry all of a sudden, but self-control of many years' training coming to his rescue. "I hope you will accept my greatest apologies." He put his hand into her delicately gloved proffered one and shook it.

Miss Pierce finally pulled hers away, as it seemed he was not intending to release it anytime soon. She glanced up to his face from where his hand lingered for a long moment alone in the air, and looked away quickly.

"Well then, shall we return to the celebration?" she said, a little too brightly.

St. John extended his arm, turned, and led her down the short corridor and into the crowded ballroom. Despite the cold of the day, the air in the chamber had grown close as the morning advanced, and suddenly he could not bear the idea of remaining at the wedding *fête* one moment longer. He looked down at the hand resting on his arm, reached up and covered it for a moment with his own, and then turned and disappeared through the door.

She had believed that when she had a moment alone to think about it, it would make more sense to her. But now, for all intents and purposes alone with her snoring father and chattering mother and younger sister in the closed carriage on the way home from Lord and Lady Bramfield's wedding celebration, Alethea could make neither head nor tail of Mr. Pennworthy's singular proposal that morning.

For remarkably singular it had been. She had barely been introduced to the gentleman and spoken a minute with him before he had asked her, quite out of the blue, to marry him. It was not until after she told him what she thought of the fun he was making of her and saw the stricken expression on his face that Alethea had started to doubt her own intuition. By then it had been too late. He had followed her wishes and taken her without hesitation back to the party. He was the consummate gentleman.

She had known that before they met today. No one, she had once heard Cassandra say, had ever suffered insult from him; he had never been known to cut anyone—although he did not particularly care for the gaming or tulip sets; and his friends were of the best sort. Why, Cassandra's new husband, the viscount Bramfield, was one of the kindest, most upright men of Alethea's acquaintance. The Earl of Alverston was another. She had never before spoken with Mr. Pennworthy, but how could a man whose reputation was so spotless and whose companions were so worthy not be a true gentleman?

She had never before spoken to him, true; *they* had never spoken to *each other.* But *he* had spoken to *her.* Six years ago, four memorable words.

He would not remember it. It had been summertime, at one of her grandparents' house parties in Kent. She had sneaked down to the hall with her sister, Octavia, and her friend, Belinda Wisterly, to peek through the banister at the guests making their way into the ballroom for the final event of the two-week-long party. They had marveled over the women in their stunning gowns and jewels, giggled at the gentlemen in their formal black satin knee-breeches, and wished themselves six years older. They had not been able to drag themselves away even when the hall emptied and the music lilted toward them from the partially drawn doors of the ball-room.

Then *he* had wandered into the hall, looking for all the world as if he were strolling aimlessly on a summer hilltop instead of where he was. Alethea's sister had giggled—she had been nine at the time, a giggling age—and he had looked up and espied them behind the banister. Not one to take her admonishments sitting down, Alethea had risen, feeling the joy of the evening slip away as she anticipated the handsome gentleman's rebuke.

But then his brows had risen, and he had

cocked his head as if suddenly hearing the strains of the set being played in the ballroom beyond. He had looked up the stairs directly at her, extended his gloved hand, and with a smile said, "Dance, madam?"

It had been a silly girl's fantasy, quickly effected and more quickly forgotten, most likely, by the playful young gentleman who had taken it into his mind to offer the nursery set a bit of diversion during what was probably for him an otherwise long and dull evening. Grandmother and Grandfather were not known to invite numerous available young ladies to their summer parties.

But the dance had been Alethea's first dance with a gentleman, and a girl at thirteen does not easily forget such an event. When it was over—and she was certain it was too soon—he had bowed deeply over her hand held lightly in his, and had said most sincerely, "Thank you." Then he had looked up to the banister, winked at the other children, and had strolled away into the ballroom again. Alethea had not said one word to him the entire time. Her heart, achingly full, had been too big to get words past.

She had reacted rather quickly this morning, she admitted now to herself as the carriage jumbled and jolted over a pothole on the city street. Her father snorted in his sleep. Her mother and Octavia, embroiled in gossip, noticed not at all.

She had assumed he was making sport of her, but perhaps she had been wrong. He was, after all, often thought to be rather . . . *eccentric*, to put it nicely. Accomplished as he was at sport, extraordinarily wealthy, and highly respected by his gentlemen friends, still there were those—and they were not few—in Society who sometimes whispered that Mr. St. John Pennworthy was perhaps a bit weak in the head.

He *must* have been playing a prank. Even a simpleton would not ask a girl he had never met, and whose parents had not betrothed him to her, to marry him in such a fashion, at the wedding breakfast of their friends. It must have been sport. How could it be otherwise?

Of course it was sport! They had not been formally introduced before this morning. He had not been in Town the previous Season, her first; his brother having died at sea the previous winter, his family had been in mourning. She had expected she would meet him some time or another, but had not thought about him in so long that their introduction this morning had taken her quite by surprise. After, that is, that peculiar look he had given her in the church. And, of course, her defenses had been up. Bertram Fenton had seen to that quite nicely.

Alethea shifted in her seat to stare out the tiny window at the drab of the London day beyond. The street was gray and wet, the low sky hung with sooty clouds. The scene was as gray as her mood had suddenly turned. She had hoped this morning's celebration would have jolted her out of her blue devils. The wedding had succeeded at this, for a short while at least. Who could resist the sunny good nature of Cassandra and her jovial viscount? Marriage certainly made lovers sparkle, did it not? Alethea thought with a twisted grin.

Marriage.

Prank or not, Mr. Pennworthy's unusual proposal, coming in the wake as it did of Bertram Fenton's betrayal and her three weeks of consequent suffering and mulling, had decided her this morning on one, definite thing: Marriage to a man—no matter who the man, be he faithless or feeble—was no longer, by any stretch of her heart's imagination, a desired attainment for Miss Alethea Pierce. She would flirt, she would dance, she would enjoy the occasional attentions of gentlemen as they came her way, but she would never, ever marry.

Two

"I am packed, and my secretary has everything in order, finally. I should be off."

Valentine Monroe, the Earl of Alverston, was sitting in one of his friend St. John's most comfortable wingback chairs by a warmly crackling fire in the tastefully furnished parlor of an elegant house on a fashionable London square. He could not wait to get home. His wife was increasing, his sister, who was presently living with them in the country, was in an ill humor these days, and he was sick and tired of London winter weather. The Regency Bill business and Bramfield's wedding both taken care of, he was anxious to return to Alverston Hall and his family.

But all was not well with his friend Pennworthy. He could read the man as easily as he had been able to read him when they were at Magdalen together a decade ago. St. John's face—and Valentine's, too, for that matter—sported more fine lines than it had ten years ago, and like his friends, Pennworthy had more responsibilities than he could have even dreamed of at that time during their halcyon days as students. But it was unlike St. John to be so blue-deviled, Lord Alverston thought. He was usually quite an even-tempered fellow.

Valentine searched his mind for something to say, afraid that nothing he could offer would take away the lingering pain that St. John must be feeling over the loss of his brother a year earlier, for that must be what was lowering his spirits. But the earl was unaccustomed to having to find things to talk about with St. John. The man was normally so conversible that Lord Alverston had never even considered it before.

"You should go back home, St. John," he finally said. "Your family is probably wondering where you are these days. And you don't have a foolish excuse like Parliament to keep you away from the country."

St. John swiveled the liquid in the glass in his hand. He stared sightlessly out the window behind the earl at the gloomy day.

"I suppose I ought to tell you," he said dully, "Prinny has offered me a title." He swiveled the wine again.

Valentine sat up straighter. "By God, has he? And how much have you had to lend him this time?"

That got a rise out of the blond man. The earl watched his friend's mouth curve into a slow grin. Pennworthy gestured with his chin toward the fire.

"I told him I would give him part ownership in the coal mine," he said, "but that enticement did not suit his fastidious nature, nor his wardrobe. 'Don't fancy the 'Change, you know.' " St. John sighed lightly. Valentine was himself grinning now. "So I sold the whole lot to a fat buyer and gave the proceeds to my future sovereign as a gift. At five percent, of course," he added, glancing at the earl. "The mine *was* a dirty business, in more than one way." There was a moment of silence, and then both men broke into laughter.

It felt good to laugh, St. John thought as his chuckles abated and the dullness descended on him again with inevitable swiftness. He looked across to his friend and nodded.

"I shan't keep you any longer, old man." He stood. "If I were fortunate enough to be married to a lady as lovely as your countess, I would hurry home myself." He extended his hand, and the earl stood and shook it.

"Thank you for your hospitality, my friend. I am glad not to have had to stir the staff to take the Holland covers off everything at Alverston House for only myself. It has been a pleasure bunking with you here." Lord Alverston kept the concern that he felt out of his voice, believing that it would not be welcomed by Pennworthy. He grasped the man's hand tightly, released it, and strode to the door beside his friend.

St. John let him out himself. Before walking down the front steps to join his valet in the waiting carriage on the street, the earl looked into his old friend's face intently.

"It is difficult to lose a brother, I know, St. John," he said soberly. "No matter how far apart you may have been, it leaves a space in you that can never be filled."

The blond man nodded, and Lord Alverston turned and stepped down to his carriage. St. John went into his house again, making his way slowly to the room he and his friend had just vacated. The footman left standing in the hall, holding the glass of sherry his master had distractedly handed him before opening the door for the earl, headed toward the kitchen, this sort of thing being not in the least bit unusual.

Moving toward the parlor window, St. John put his hand up to the cold pane of glass and imagined he could feel the dampness right through the smooth surface. He could not really, of course. His own Venetian glass factory had produced this fine specimen, but he felt no pleasure in its perfection today. He dropped his hand, raising his other to sip his sherry. Nothing met his lips, and he flexed his empty fingers in irritation.

Woolgathering again. Long, extended woolgathering. His heart was clearly not in much of anything these days. It was a sorry day when a man could not even keep his head clear enough to ensure that his own hand kept his drink.

St. John stepped over to the sideboard and poured himself another glass of sweet wine. Leaning against the massive piece of furniture, he sipped the sherry, tasting the syrupy liquid not at all. He was sorry Valentine had noticed his downheartedness. But the fellow was a good friend; what could St. John expect living under the same roof with him for these past days?

Of course, it wasn't so much the space left in his heart by the loss of Jacob that troubled him now. St. John knew that place would never be filled. But St. John had grieved long for Jacob, and knew that his little brother was now in a better place. Then he had begun his life again, and had encouraged his family to do the same.

No, the problem was that other space, the vast one that was supposed to be filled with the affection of a wife for the rest of his days. It was the one he had been ignoring for a decade of his life so that he could make of himself something she would be proud of and wish to have as her own. And now that he had, the lady did not seem to want him. Or at least the lady he had sworn was supposed to be the one he asked.

He had felt so certain when he had looked at her, felt such a direct rightness in the brief touch of her hand upon his arm, even after she had rejected him. Somehow he wanted to believe that such indicators pointed to her, no matter that he'd never met her before the day of the wedding. It was not magic, or some other such nonsense, just pure confidence in the way it was intended to be. St. John had never supposed that when he saw the girl he should marry he would not recognize her right away. And he had always fully expected that when the time came that he knew he was completely prepared in all of the ways that mattered to take a wife, that the right wife would somehow be presented to him. It had been as simple as that. How could it possibly have gone wrong? Given the years he had spent in careful preparation, it was unthinkable.

St. John set the crystal glass down on the sideboard and crossed his arms over his tastefully embroidered waistcoat. Perhaps he had asked the wrong one?

No, he was certain she was the right one, had

been from the moment he'd seen her there in St. George's. Miss Pierce. Miss Alethea Pierce. Even her name sounded right to him. But perhaps he was mistaken.

Whatever the case, she had rejected him, had thought he was playing some sort of practical joke on her, and had told him so in no uncertain terms. St. John never contradicted a lady. He had retreated behind his mask of breeding, tucking away his heart for another day, and had escorted her back to the party.

Now he would have to find another bride, he supposed glumly. He did not truly want to after this first—and what he had always imagined would be the only—attempt to marry. But married he was going to be. And he would be betrothed by tomorrow if it was the last thing he did. He had promised himself that years ago.

St. John had been waiting impatiently for tomorrow—his thirtieth birthday—for as long as he could remember. His older sister had told him he should come celebrate with her and Michael and the children at their house since he was in Town. His stepmother had written, telling him to come home in time for the day. His young half sisters had lovingly postscripted that they missed him and wanted to be the first to wish him happy.

He had wanted to insist they all wish him happy, and not because he was finally turning thirty years old, but because he had his betrothed on his arm to introduce to them all. Long ago he had promised himself he would be betrothed by the night of his thirtieth birthday. When he had proposed to Miss Pierce only days before, he had thought things were going as planned, as desired.

He had wanted for so long to be married. He had watched his friends, one by one, tying the knot, envious of their happiness, waiting for the day his own would begin. The night before Bramfield's wedding, at a small gathering of the Regent and some of his cronies, Prinny had taken St. John aside and told him the news of his impending preferment. It was the final building block in a castle he had painstakingly erected for himself and his someday bride. Would that he knew now who she was supposed to be. When he had seen Miss Pierce there across the church aisle, he had felt so *certain* . . .

St. John pushed himself away from the sideboard and strode across the room to the door. If he were going to be betrothed by tomorrow, he could not stand about moping. He had quick work to do.

Two weeks yet until the Season began, but, in truth, St. John was feeling not too terribly desperate about his lack of a bride. Only just a little.

His thirtieth birthday came and went, but his sister Amelia, with whose family he had celebrated the day, had assured him that the best time to meet unmarried ladies was the very beginning of any Season. Girls right out of the schoolroom were especially susceptible to the charms of interested gentlemen. If he was so set on finding a bride soon—and Amelia intimated to him that she did not quite understand his hurry—he ought to ingratiate himself with the mothers and aunts and other miscellaneous chaperones of these newly budding Blossoms of Society. He was sure to be accepted.

Waiting was not easy, but he respected his sister's opinion, and knew there was some truth in what she said. St. John had not told her of Miss Pierce's rejection. It had not seemed honorable, seeing that it was Miss Pierce's business as much as his own. But Amelia had understood that he was not entirely confident of being accepted should he be so fortunate as to find an appropriate girl.

In truth, Miss Pierce's refusal had left him feeling quite out of sorts for the past several weeks. After the Earl of Alverston's departure, St. John had resumed his normal activities in Town: driving; visiting his club, Jackson's Tattersall's; business at the Exchange; fencing; riding along Rotten Row; attending the theater and the occasional cockfight; and, naturally, checking in at the Docks regularly. He had even frequented a few discreet gaming houses in order to distract himself from unbidden thoughts. In any case, that manner of diversion was expected of him, although he did it as infrequently as possible.

He could afford it, of course. He could afford to lose at the tables every night for a year and still be standing on his feet. He simply found no pleasure in it. As he found little pleasure—of a *lasting* sort—in that other activity in which gentlemen of his stature were expected to engage. He had learned, in the end, to cultivate the Corinthian style in order to avoid just that sort of thing. A man truly engrossed in his horses and carriages could not spend undue amounts of time gambling or lightskirting, could he?

During the past weeks he had avoided most of the pre-season *soirées* for which he received cards. His heart was not in them. The desire to wed was warring painfully inside him with the newly acquired and unwelcome certainty that somehow he never would. The beginning of the Season would be time enough, he told himself.

There was one invitation he could not ignore, however, out of deference to his parents. Thus one early spring evening that seemed more like winter, he donned his elegantly understated evening garb and made his way to the Town home of the people who had been his neighbors in the countryside his entire life. St. John had been playmates with their second son Charles in childhood, and his stepmother had written him from the countryside that she and Mr. Pennworthy regretted not being able to attend the Strapleys' fortieth wedding anniversary *fête;* wouldn't he be so kind as to present himself in their stead?

St. John arrived at a fashionable hour. He gifted a footman with his overcoat and hat, and made his way into what proved to be a rather impressive crush for what had been advertised as a simple pre-season supper party.

"Darling St. John!" he heard exclaimed in rapturous tones as he approached his host and hostess. Mrs. Strapley grasped his hands with her own excessively soft ones and he brought them to his lips briefly. "Or should I say rather, Sir St. John?" She laughed expressively and St. John could not help but smile. Mrs. Strapley had always been something of a melodramaticist, albeit a charming one. He felt his host pat him affectionately on the shoulder and turned to the older man.

"We're proud of you, son. Congratulations on the baronetcy," Strapley beamed as if St. John were his own progeny.

"Sir, madam, you are too kind. I congratulate you on your many years of happy marriage, and in their stead bear to you my parents' good wishes as well," he said with what sounded to him impressive calm. To compliment them on four decades of successful wedded bliss cost him no little effort.

Niceties shortly over with, St. John wandered into the drawing room to await dinner, chatting here and there with acquaintances as he went. Shortly, he caught the eye of Charles Strapley and greeted his boyhood friend with pleasure.

"You've been in Town for some time now, haven't you, St. John? What's brought and kept you here?" the shorter man questioned amiably. All of the Strapleys were short and amiable.

"Oh, business, what have you," he replied noncommittally.

"I heard Bramfield's wedding was a fine affair, as those things go. Did you kiss the bride, old fellow?"

St. John grinned slightly, as was expected of him, but he cringed inside. Could a conversation never exclude mention of a wedding?

"Lady Bramfield is very gracious," he managed. "I expect you will meet her once the couple has returned from their wedding trip and my parents are in Town again. They intend to throw a rout in the newlyweds' honor." He searched around for something else to talk about, aware that Charles seemed perversely intent on pursuing the topic. "Ah, I see your sister. Are all of your siblings present tonight?"

Bland but comfortable topic. He thought.

"Yes, all of them. Felicia is the only unmarried one of the lot, of course—except for me, that is," Charles said with the ever-present laugh. "You missed Patricia's wedding last summer, but you recall Dora and Elizabeth have both been married for several years. I have three nephews and two nieces already, in addition to my brother's heir."

"Of course, I remember your sisters' weddings well." Of course he did; he always remembered occasions on which he wanted to cry. St. John had wanted to cry on both of those occasions. Not because he wished *himself* to marry the brides—they were both somewhat short for his considerable height, albeit very nice girls—but because he always wanted to cry at weddings. He never had, naturally. "I am glad to hear the family is growing so successfully."

"Come, let us join Felicia," Charles said, turning toward his young sister. "She will be delighted to see you. She mustn't have been out of the schoolroom the last time you saw her."

As they approached the girl standing amidst a group of young men and women, St. John noted to her brother that he had known her during her Come Out Season two years ago. How lovely she had grown, too, he thought with a critical eye. Short blond ringlets framed a pleasant and friendly face, eyes sparkling with the attention she was obviously receiving from several of the young gentlemen around her. She was almost what St. John would have called radiant. But not quite. Very pretty, though. She was, additionally, somewhat taller than her sisters Dora and Elizabeth. Why had he not before considered her in this light?

Because two years ago he had not been looking.

"St. John!" she exclaimed prettily when he and her brother reached the group, and she extended her gloved hand to him. "It has been quite an age, has it not?" Her voice was lively, affectionate. St. John felt something inside him, something that had been subdued for several weeks now, stir.

"Miss Strapley, you are lovelier this evening than I have even remembered." He smiled into the girl's bright eyes, wholly unaware of the quick intakes of breath of at least two of the other maidens standing nearby as he did so. Mr. Charles Strapley noticed, and adroitly made Pennworthy acquainted with them. St. John graciously bowed to each one and made the appropriate remarks, but Miss Felicia Strapley captivated his attention.

Throughout the remainder of the party, he circulated among his friends and acquaintances, even danced after supper with several young ladies. He kept his eye on Miss Strapley, however, the conviction slowly growing in him that perhaps this evening he had discovered his bride.

It was not the same conviction he had felt with Lady Bramfield's wedding attendant, but it was a secure feeling, nonetheless. He had known Felicia Strapley her entire life, remembered her as a tiny child and then as an awkward adolescent.

Now she was a pretty, spirited young lady. She
had always been fond of him, and he of her. And
if she married him, she would remain close to
her family home and their children could be
raised with both sets of grandparents conveniently located. He understood this might not be
sufficient enticement to become his wife, but he
could hope.

He was not able to speak with her again at her
parents' party, but during the next weeks St.
John managed several times to engage himself
very neatly in activities that included Miss Felicia
Strapley and her brother. He could never seem
to meet her alone, however, and as his courage
increased so, too, did his frustration. He supposed it was to his benefit that Felicia could become accustomed to him; after his first attempt,
he suspected the surprise approach was not a
particularly successful one. Nonetheless, it was
with considerable irritation that when he finally
arranged one day to take her driving in his new
curricle out to Richmond Park, a Mr. Frederick
Charleston put in his twopence and suggested
they make a party of it. It was, in St. John's humble opinion, much too cold yet to take a picnic
into the countryside, but since Miss Felicia
Strapley seemed to be amenable to the idea, he
went along with it. They had been surrounded
by friends all day long.

Thus it was not until a full two weeks after
meeting her again that he finally found the occasion for private speech with her. It was at the
first ball of the Season, hosted by Lord and Lady
Martindale, on behalf of their youngest daughter's Come Out. With the entire *ton* returned to

Town finally, it was destined to be a sad crush. St. John attended solely to claim a promised set from Miss Felicia Strapley and hopefully to make his proposal while he had her for once all to himself.

"Why, St. John, you dance divinely!" Felicia sparkled up at him as he led her around the crowded ballroom as best he could, given the large number of couples sharing the space with them. She was fully aware of the jealous glances being thrown in her direction not only from her unpartnered friends on the edges of the dance floor, but also from certain young maidens less enviably paired in the dance. Felicia smiled ever more brightly at the handsome, newly titled baronet. It would be too soon that she would no longer be able to garner the envy of her friends like this so easily, and she was one to take every advantage offered to her.

"I am certain we have danced before, Miss Felicia," he replied evenly. "Did I not lead you out a number of times two years ago during your Come Out?"

"Oh, St. John, of course you did," she giggled. "But never for a minuet. I am so very impressed how you manage to make these dull-as-dishwater patterns *diverting!* And you *must* stop calling me *Miss* Felicia. Why, we have known each other these ages!"

St. John looked down into her rosy-cheeked visage and appreciated the high spirits evident in her expression. She seemed especially lively this evening. Now was a good time. The dance would keep them together for many minutes yet.

"Felicia," he began, not unsure in the least of

what he was about to utter. "We have known each other for ages, indeed, but you are not the same girl you were just a few years ago."

She batted her golden lashes and her cheeks dimpled. "Is that a compliment, Sir St. John Pennworthy? You are too kind."

"I wish to be more than kind, Felicia. I wish, in fact, that you would consent to be my bride."

Felicia Strapley's mouth fell wide open, but it was to her credit that she continued to dance quite adequately as she stared at him in shock. When she found her tongue, it was to exclaim:

"Why, St. John, I cannot!"

Sir St. John Pennworthy appeared nonplussed. "You do not *wish* to? You *will* not?" He thought he ought to understand perfectly. Their longtime familiarity caused him to speak as he ought not.

"I *cannot!*" Felicia's cheeks had paled, and her mouth had closed into an earnest pout. "You see I have just this week accepted Mr. Charleston. I daresay I was terribly happy about it until this very moment."

"Mr. Charleston?" St. John said blankly.

"Frederick Charleston! You *know*, St. John! You met him last week at Mrs. Granville's musical evening. He courted me last Season, you see, and Papa finally consented to let him offer for me this Season as long as we kept it between the families for the first few weeks. My grandfather is opposed to the match, on account of Frederick not having very high expectations. Since Grandfather is in failing health, Papa wishes us to prepare him slowly for the news. Frederick is a fourth son, you know, but he has found a living recently and will be a curate soon enough if we are fortunate. It is what encouraged him to finally speak with my father again." She seemed to recall herself suddenly, and turned her distressed gaze up to him, willing the empty expression on his face to alter. She would scold herself for weeks for having flirted with him so shamelessly tonight.

"St. John! I am so very fond of you, you know. I do not know how to thank you for your offer." Her voice was plaintive.

St. John had heard little of what she said, or rather, he had heard it all, but had not bothered to really listen. He looked soberly down at her troubled visage.

"You need not thank me, Felicia. We are friends, and shall remain so. May I take this opportunity to congratulate you on your betrothal?"

He both watched and heard her sigh in grand relief. She was quite like her mother, actually. He had never really noticed that before.

"Oh, thank you, St. John! You are too kind. And you will keep my arrangement with Frederick a secret until it is safe to let Grandfather know?" Her bright eyes entreated.

"Indeed, I shall," he replied evenly. She looked up at him, suddenly subdued for a girl of her age and nature.

"And I shall keep your offer to myself, St. John. I am most, most gratified by it."

Gratification he could do without, St. John thought to himself as he walked slowly from the ballroom after having deposited Felicia with a jealously fuming betrothed standing at the edge of the dance floor. *Acceptance* he would have ap-

preciated very much, thank you. Raising his hand
to alert a footman that he was in need of his
coat and hat, St. John caught the eye of a lady
standing a short distance away. His own widened.

It was she.

He nodded and watched Miss Pierce make a
bare curtsy to him. Then he took his belongings
from the waiting footman and walked out into
the cold March night. The heels of his shining
evening shoes clicked desolately on the pavement
as he moved into the middle of the dim, lamp-lit
street and headed for his own empty house. A
house, he mused gloomily, bound to remain
empty indefinitely now.

Three

Alethea watched him go, wondering if his despondency was apparent to everyone who looked at him, or only to her. She thought that perhaps she had an advantage over others, however. She was certain she had seen that look on his face once before: over a month ago, when she had told him just what she had thought of his unexpected proposal.

But if he was despondent, he hid it quite well. He had departed with broad shoulders very straight, smiles for several acquaintances she saw him pass on his way out, and even a few pleasant words for their hostess behind whom Alethea and her companions were standing. He did not *seem* despondent in the usual way. Perhaps it was her imagination. It was just that his eyes looked so very odd.

Of course, that might be their usual expression. Despite a niggling guilt, at tea tables and during afternoon strolls over the past several weeks, she had subtly encouraged gossip about the man in order to learn more about him than she had already known when he proposed to her. It was simply more of the same, however, she was disappointed to find. No one had anything new to say about him. He was thought to be a little *phlegmatic.* On the other hand, he was a bruising rider and a whip of no little expertise. He was a member of both the Whip Club and the Four-in-Hand Club, the latter which he had been invited into just shortly after he received his title, perhaps not so coincidentally. Most important, when it came to gossip about him, however, a key question arose. "All of that delicious money had to come from somewhere, did it not?" Those had been the words of Lady Charity Chetham, whose beautiful daughter had not yet nabbed a husband after two Seasons, and who herself was everything less than the virtue her name suggested. In any case, St. John Pennworthy had not come upon his fortune accidentally. He had made it himself.

Many turned up their noses at the smell of Shop about him and flatly refused to socialize with him. Others recognized well enough that he did not himself work in the factories, most of which were on the Continent, after all. He did have quite a bit of land to his name, from which came the bulk of his income, including a perfectly unexceptionable plantation in the Colonies.

Still others borrowed money from him so often that they could not help but consider him part of their set. In truth, Almack's was the only door in Town still closed to him. Alethea was not alone in thinking privately that this was to his great advantage. He had been invited to so many of the *ton* functions for so many years that by now it did not signify anymore how he had made his fortune. And those hostesses who still felt the least little bit of hesitation when adding the attractive if eccentric favorite to their guest lists comforted themselves with the recollection that he *was* the great-grandson of an earl, after all.

St. John Pennworthy was an anomaly, that was for certain. Alethea turned back to her friends, her thoughts troubled. Then her heart jumped.

He had joined the group, and he was looking straight at her with rather piercing intensity.

Desperate, Alethea turned to her friend standing next to her and pretended to have torn a flounce during the last set. As she hurried away from the group in which Bertram Fenton stood, she knew she had narrowly escaped his attentions yet once again. But he would corner her eventually, of that she was certain.

"Alethea, you cannot run away from him forever." Miss Wisterly had just straightened up from discovering that her friend's flounces were in perfectly good order. She put her hands on her gingham-clad hips and gazed impatiently at Alethea. "You share the same set and you are bound to be forced to speak with him someday, you know. Why not let that someday be sooner than later and get the unpleasantness out of the way?"

Alethea turned from her friend and gazed into the mirror at her own reflection. There were several other ladies in the chamber, all engaged in animated gossiping. Her conversation with Miss Wisterly was effectively private.

"I do not know why it cannot be later," she

mumbled, unaccustomed to being so fainthearted and not liking it in the least. She examined her red-brown hair in the glass, twined into an artful S-curve at the nape of her neck. Until she had seen Bertram Fenton among the crowd, she had felt positively attractive this evening. Come to think of it, she had stopped thinking about what a lovely time she was having—enjoying the attentions of a number of young gentlemen—*not* when she had seen Bertram, but when she had noticed Sir Pennworthy leave. Perhaps had she not been so distracted by that gentleman's apparent dejection she would have been able to react to Mr. Fenton's sudden appearance with some semblance of calm.

"Later is now, Alethea." Belinda sat down on the embroidered stool beside her friend and looked into the mirror at Alethea's unsettled features. "Won't you tell me what it was that happened? I could shoot myself for not being here when whatever it was took place!"

Alethea winced involuntarily, and then patted her friend on her wrist.

"But you don't know how to shoot straight, Lindy, so what would that be worth in the end?" She grinned, and Miss Wisterly's pink lips cracked a smile, but her eyes still questioned. Alethea felt her stomach tighten.

How could she tell Belinda when she could barely bring herself to think about it? It wasn't that she could not recall in vivid detail every moment of the nightmarish betrayal; indeed, the images were marked on her memory in lurid colors. It was that she did not wish to expose herself for being such a fool. At least, not expose herself more than she was already exposed.

Alethea winced again. Poor choice of words.

She had never before seen another woman's bared bosom, and wished she could erase the image she had of the unique instance. And erase the image of the woman's raised skirts, the sound of her breathy voice repeating his name, and especially the triumphant glint in her eyes when she had seen Alethea in the glass from across the room. It had been dark in the doorway where she had come upon them unexpectedly, but the other girl had known whose gasp of dismay she heard. *He* had been too involved in his lechery to hear Alethea's unconscious utterance of shock. Thank heaven!

Alethea could not imagine it was in Sylvia Sinclaire's interests to inform Mr. Fenton that they had been caught out. With her golden beauty and ample dowry, Miss Sinclaire was setting her sights rather higher than a mere second son, Alethea thought with bitterness. She would leave Bertram, used and discarded, to Miss Alethea Pierce with pleasure—after, of course, she had taken hers with him.

Alethea's eyes burned. She blinked, bringing herself back to the small, well-appointed chamber in the Martindales' elegant town house. She was beginning to feel as miserable as Sir Pennworthy had looked earlier, and that simply would not do.

She turned to Miss Wisterly, a firm smile on her lips.

"Belinda, I shall tell you another time, if there is occasion to," she said. "Now, however, I believe I would like to enjoy the remainder of the evening. Captain Gilford asked me to reserve the next set for him, and I am quite of a mind not to keep him waiting." She stood and moved out of the room. Her friend followed her with misgiving.

"You say you enjoy the hunt, Sir St. John? I am so very gratified to hear it! If only more young gentlemen would admit to their love of it, we ladies should more often have the occasion to join in the excitement as well."

St. John was strolling along a footpath in Hyde Park, on his arm Lady Agatha Boxbottom, the daughter of the baroness Boxbottom, one of his aunt's especial intimates. Those two elder ladies were taking their exercise in the comfortably cushioned confines of a rather old-fashioned but exceedingly well-preserved barouche. The barouche, to St. John's initial chagrin, was following him and his walking companion along at a short distance. Lady Agatha never took exercise unless on foot or on horseback. The young lady herself had informed him of this quite directly just the previous evening. She loathed carriages, revealing to him the definite conviction that they encouraged the waste of good horseflesh. St. John had made a mental note to omit from his conversation with her any mention of the dozen or so conveyances gracing his various liveries across England and the Continent at the present time.

"I enjoy it very much, Lady Agatha. I have some extraordinarily fine hunters in my stables in Hertford. The terrain is quite excellent there."

It was a fine day for early April, the sun peeking through light, high clouds as if it actually meant to make a visit of some length with the earth. St. John breathed in a deep breath of spring air. If he had stopped for a moment to ponder it, he might have imagined he was enjoying himself.

"Splendid!" Lady Agatha said little that did not warrant an exclamatory tone. "I would very much like to experience it someday, Sir St. John! Hertford is not so far from one of my father's properties. I shall make arrangements to be there the next time you call a hunt. Shall we agree upon it?"

She turned to face him and St. John marveled at her forthrightness, so unusual in a girl of only twenty-two years. She would never hide an engagement with another man; she would not know why she ought. He found this characteristic very refreshing. And she was attractive, rather handsome, in truth, with strong yet well-balanced features and short, raven black curls. Certainly she carried herself excellently, as if always on horseback. He could come to like this young lady quite nicely.

"We shall, my lady." St. John nodded and she tucked her hand more firmly in his elbow; they continued on their way down the path in excellent accord with each other.

Some minutes later, they approached an intersection with a carriage path. Lady Agatha was embarking on an account of her father's latest stud purchase when a conveyance, pulled swiftly by two showy grays, rattled to a sudden halt not fif-

teen yards in front of them and abruptly discharged a lady onto the path.

St. John and his companion stopped in their
tracks, unable to hear what was being said between the driver of the phaeton and the woman
in the road. But whatever it was, the tones of
the two voices were far from congenial. They
watched as the man angrily thrust the reins into
the hands of his tiger and made as if to alight
from the carriage as well. The lady looked desperately about her, and, seeing their party at a
close distance, began to walk swiftly toward
them. She held a scrap of white linen to her
mouth and her head was bent slightly, obscuring
her face behind her bonnet. Nonetheless, St.
John recognized her.

The angry gentleman took the reins in his
hands again, whipped up his grays, and drove off
at a mighty speed up the road.

"Cow-handed clunch!" St. John heard Lady
Agatha exclaim beside him and, brows rising, he
turned to regard her for a thoughtful moment.
Then, returning his attention to the figure
quickly approaching them, he gently disengaged
his arm from Lady Agatha's hold and stepped
forward to meet the young lady on the path.

When she neared him, she finally looked up.
Her mouth made an "O" as her expressive hazel
eyes widened.

"Oh! Sir! I—"

"Miss Pierce," he said in an even tone. "May
I and my companions be of some assistance to
you?" Would she always look at him as if he had
just walked out of Bedlam?

His voice held nothing but concern, and

Alethea felt her racing heart begin to slow. She dabbed at her reddened, running nose with her ineffectual scrap of lace, afraid to draw it away for the mess she must make. Without a word, Sir Pennworthy reached into his waistcoat and withdrew a small square of pressed linen and held it out to her. Alethea took it quickly and mopped up her streaming face.

"Sir," she finally said, realizing that the baronet's lady companion was standing diffidently not many yards away, unwilling to approach them. "You are very kind. I wonder if I could trouble you—"

"Miss Pierce!" The voice came from the carriage that was just pulling to a halt behind St. John, and he watched as the girl turned her mottled face to his aunt.

"You have been abominably used, I can see." Lady Fitzwarren's groom handed her out of the barouche with no little effort, but the countess moved more quickly forward than the extraordinary bulk of her peacock-blue taffeta walking gown would have seemed to allow. She put herself between her nephew and Alethea and took the girl's hands into both of her own. "You are fortunate that this has occurred at such an early hour. There are few about to remark it, but you have undoubtedly done wisely to leave that jackanapes to take himself off from where he came, which will stand you in good stead this evening in clubs and drawing rooms, if I am not mistaken."

St. John watched Miss Pierce's lips tremble, but then she bit them as if willing herself to be resolute, and took a deep breath. He did not allow himself to smile.

"Now come with me and we shall make you quite comfortable in my carriage," his aunt continued, leading the girl toward the barouche. "May I present you to Lady Boxbottom, a very dear, dear old friend of mine"—Did Alethea mistake the meaning in those words, that neither Lady Fitzwarren nor her friend would tell tales of what they had witnessed?—"and her daughter, Lady Agatha, who is taking the air with St. John." She bustled Alethea up into the carriage. "What a magnificent day it is, don't you agree, Miss Pierce? I was just telling Margaret that I have not seen such an April day since I was a girl in my first seasons like you. It augurs ill for the summer heat to come, but no mind, especially for you young ones. Ah to be young again! Now there, I am immensely delighted that we have happened upon you, in particular. There are details of your cousin Juliet's impending ball that I am quite anxious to hear about firsthand—"

The barouche jolted into languorous motion, St. John extended his arm for Lady Agatha once more, and they continued down the path. The addition of Miss Pierce to their party had not ruffled his companion in the least, he was interested to note, and she took up where their conversation had left off with remarkable perseverance.

It was only when he was climbing the front steps of his house an hour later that he realized he had not attended to a word of what Lady Agatha had told him regarding her father's stud, nor anything else that she had said after that.

For that matter, he could not remember a word of what he himself had said to Lady Agatha following their unexpected meeting with Miss Pierce on the path. He imagined it was quite likely that he had said nothing at all.

Four

"Whatever possessed you to agree to drive out with him in the first place, dearest? And without your maid?" Winifred Pierce's question was something of an exclamation.

Alethea was sitting in her mother's dressing room; that constitutionally nervous woman reclined incommodiously but decorously upon a claw-footed chaise whose upholstery perfectly matched the tinted burnt-crimson hue of its occupant's carefully arranged hair. Fifteen-year-old Octavia was stretched out nearby in an equally spindly chair, her thin, adolescent legs dangling over an arm. The girl giggled, and Alethea pursed her lips.

"I think she had no other choice, Mrs. Pierce. Mr. Fenton has been pestering her a great deal." The voice came from the window embrasure where Belinda Wisterly perched with her arms crossed, her expression pensive. She met her friend's gaze. "If Alethea would only tell us about *what* she needed to speak to Mr. Fenton, however, we might be able to get to the bottom of this." Her eyes narrowed, and Alethea set her jaw. She had known it would come to this.

"So be it. I shall tell you."

"Octavia, do run away now. I shall call you back if I need you." Mrs. Pierce's voice was light but still brooked no disagreement.

"But, Mama," the younger girl protested, sitting upright in the chair, "I ought to be allowed to stay. Thea will tell me everything afterward anyway. She always does."

Not this time, Little Sister, Alethea thought miserably. There were some things a girl had to learn on her own, or not at all. Mrs. Pierce shooed her younger daughter from the room, and Belinda moved from the window box to the chair by the fireplace. Before her courage waned, Alethea launched into her tale. It was an abbreviated version; she could not fully admit to the extent of the secret promises she and Bertram Fenton had made to each other before his awful betrayal, nor say aloud the things she had actually seen that night. Even describing the situation in the barest terms brought the blush to her cheeks most unbearably. But her mother and Belinda took her meaning.

"You mean to say you thought that you could simply tell Mr. Fenton you had seen this—this *tableau,* that this discovery was what had turned your affections away from him so suddenly, and he would simply take the hint and disappear from your life forever?" Miss Wisterly's tone was incredulous.

Alethea shrugged, still not convinced she had done wrong. She felt much better for finally having confronted him.

"He is *supposed* to be a gentleman, Lindy. I

thought he would have to accept my explanation, however much he did not like it."

He had not. Her defection irked him too profoundly, Alethea had learned in his carriage that morning. His complexion had gone from white to red to spotty as she told him how she had found him and Sylvia Sinclaire engaged in the library during the Easterlings' winter ball. She had used very few words, and most of her speech had been directed toward informing him that their understanding, however informal, was most definitely nullified. She ought to have anticipated his response. It had, after all, been almost three months since she had begun avoiding his company, and still he persisted in trying to win her attention.

Nevertheless, Alethea had been entirely unprepared when, after drawing to a halt behind a clump of trees in the Park, Mr. Fenton had pulled her into his arms. He had begun telling her quite stridently how much he loved her, how it had been a terrible mistake, and in any case Miss Sinclaire had lured him into it, how he had much rather make love to Alethea than that little tart. He had been trying to do just that despite her struggles when Alethea was able finally to wrest the reins from his hands and start the phaeton into motion. The restless grays pranced about, drawing Mr. Fenton's attention, and he had begun to curse both them and her as he endeavored to get them under control. When he finally did, Alethea took her life into her own hands, pulling away from him and jumping down to the path below.

It was only then that she had seen the onlookers not far away. Knowing they were her only hope—not allowing herself to think that they could present a worse fate than what she was fleeing from—she had started toward them without a thought other than to get away from Bertram Fenton. An angel had placed Sir St. John Pennworthy and his aunt in her path. Sir Pennworthy had behaved discreetly and compassionately; Lady Fitzwarren had turned the disastrous into the unremarkable.

Almost. Alethea knew this episode would be the talk of the Town for a day or two, perhaps more if nothing else came along to distract the *ton's* attention. But she did not regret it. Bertram Fenton must know now he should leave her in peace in the future, and that was what she had wanted from the interview in the first place. Her heart ached, nevertheless. The smart of his betrayal was taking a long time to heal. She had never expected a man could say one thing to a girl and mean another.

"Darling, how terribly, horrendously monstrous of him!" Her mother rose languidly from the chaise and moved to Alethea to enfold her in a warm, scented embrace. "You should have told us you and he were so fond. We might have arranged for a formal betrothal much earlier and this peccadillo with Miss Sinclaire would never have happened in the first place."

Alethea stiffened and drew away from her mother.

"It no longer signifies in the least, Mama," she said tightly, trying to control her voice more for her own sake than for the others'. "It is over and done now, and nothing can be done about it."

"Indeed," Miss Wisterly said shortly, standing. "You are better off without him, Thea, and this leaves you quite unencumbered to enjoy this Season with me." She took Alethea's hand in her own and drew her friend to her feet. "In the meanwhile, we shall behave as if this never occurred. Our friends will stand by you—you did nothing wrong—and in no time at all this will all be an insignificant memory."

Alethea knew Belinda was speaking to impress upon the biddable Mrs. Pierce that forthwith the topic would be unwelcome in conversation, as well that it should not by any means be shared with Mr. Pierce. She was grateful for the championship. But her old friend would be of little help if Bertram Fenton had not also taken the same notion.

St. John found himself in something of a fix. The previous evening at his club he had discovered in the books a wager that had unsettled him greatly: A hundred pounds wagered on whether "Mr. B. F. would bed or wed Miss A. P." before the end of the summer. The wagerers were rather loose screws, he knew, not the sort St. John ever found himself socializing with; they were particular cronies of the gentleman mentioned in the bet. The Honorable Bertram Fenton was a notorious libertine and, if rumor was to be believed, rather excessively unsportsmanlike in his dealings with the muslin company. Not honorable in the least, in fact.

Each man to his own, St. John had always believed. Until now. This time it was different. St. John did not like the open connection of the lady in question with this band of scoundrels. He had heard the rumors concerning the event in the Park, naturally. He had ignored the questions he received while carefully proffering his adjusted version of the story to only his very closest companions—which, he was certain, they immediately carried to others until the whole *ton* had heard what "truly" happened. He had assumed that would be the end of it. The wager, written in ink in the betting book at Brooks's, told otherwise.

Now, seated on one of his favorite mounts at the four-mile mark of the race he and the redoubtable Lady Agatha were attending on the Bath road this morning, St. John found himself discomfited.

The spring sunshine shone down clear and warm upon them. Conveyances were scattered about, drawn up as near to the posting-gate as was safe. They were all waiting for the three competing curricles to speed around the bend in the road three-quarters of a mile distant and meet them at the halfway point of the race. There were only a few other ladies present, most of the onlookers being male, but Lady Agatha seemed to be enjoying herself immensely. It was remarkable, really, how much pleasure she was taking in a *carriage* race.

But Lady Agatha's pleasure was not first and foremost on his mind at the moment. If he looked to his left slightly, he could bring himself face-to-face with the fellow driving the phaeton with the flashy grays. St. John had seen those grays before, just before he had seen the overset features of Miss Alethea Pierce in Hyde Park four days ago.

Mr. Bertram Fenton should be horsewhipped. If rumor was to be believed—other than St. John's own rumors, of course—the scoundrel had insulted Miss Pierce in the Park shortly before their parties had met. The man should be taken to task for it, but no one seemed to be coming forward to do the job. St. John had inquired of his aunt concerning the girl's male relatives, but Lady Fitzwarren had laughed and told him—rather curiously—to search somewhere else for a champion for his lady.

The wager made Miss Pierce's position rather more abhorrent. She had no one to defend her from the likes of Bertram Fenton and his lot. It irked St. John beyond what he was accustomed to feeling, quite violently, in fact. If it were one of his sisters in Miss Pierce's place, he would have called out the fellow immediately. He could not call out Mr. Fenton, however, for he bore no connection whatsoever to the abused lady. Recognizing this chafed.

He only became aware that Lady Agatha was trying to speak to him when he felt the tap of her riding crop on his gloved hand.

"Sir St. John! I say, this is famous sport! I am most pleased you suggested it to me!"

She was beaming, and the expression made her appear a great deal more attractive than she had seemed to him over the past several days. She had quite a spirit, too, like an excellent hunter, come to think of it. St. John smiled.

"I am happy to have done so."

In fact, she had made the suggestion herself after overhearing talk of the race at a breakfast party, which they had both attended the day before. St. John had decided then that it would be the ideal occasion to make known to her his hopes for their future together. He cleared his throat in preparation.

"My lady, there is something I wish to ask you," he began. "I would be most honored—"

"Oh, there they are now! Do look, Sir St. John! Here they come!"

Harnesses began to jingle around them. St. John let out a deep breath and directed his gaze over Lady Agatha's mount's ears to the curricles heading in their direction. Excitement suddenly tingled in the air, and voices rose amongst the onlookers as gentlemen began to call modifications of their bets to each other across the road.

"Is this not splendid? Why, it is better than Newmarket, I'll wager, here on the open road!"

St. John shifted his gaze to the handsome features of the noblewoman beside him. They were rapt with excitement. Her eyes sparkled, her cheeks were flushed, and she held her hands together so tightly he was certain she would damage her gloves if she did not take care. She was a passionate one, that was certain. St. John found himself wondering not idly if she would be so in *alternative* situations.

"Lady Agatha, I wondered if I might speak on something—"

"Lord Soames's chestnuts are magnificent, are they not?" his companion exclaimed as the carriages approached them rapidly, the dust on the road stirring wildly in their wake. St. John drew his eyes away from the young woman and directed his gaze at the leaders.

"Yes, quite magnificent—" he began, admiring the dark red-brown of the horses' coats, lathered at the withers as they strained to hold their lead.

"They will not maintain the second half at the rate Soames is pushing them to, no matter how impressive they are," he heard Lady Agatha say animatedly, but St. John was not attending. That was an especially beautiful color, it was true, particularly for a woman's hair. . . .

St. John's eyes shot open.

"Lady Agatha, may I suggest that we—"

The carriages swept by in a thundering tumult, leaving the onlookers in a cloud of fine brown dust and scrambling in preparation to take themselves off to the end point of the race before the drivers reached it first. St. John saw his companion turn her mount's head and put her heels to the mare's sides.

"Come along, Sir St. John!" she called, as she moved in the direction of the other mounted riders who were heading for a path through the woods. "We shan't want to miss the finish!"

Urging his mount to a canter and then a gallop, St. John followed along in the dust as best he could.

"What you need is a ring, sir. A nice, sparkling ring would do the trick right and tight."

St. John was sitting in his most comfortable chair in the most comfortable room in his house, his dressing room, the room he most often sought to find peace and quiet. He was watching his valet brush free of copious dirt his new bright yellow striped and spotted waistcoat. It was not a week since he had received it from the tailor, but after this morning's activities it looked as if he had owned it for years. He had thought Lady Agatha, given her unexpected conversion to curricle racing the day before, would be impressed by the uniform of the Four-in-Hand Club that he had sported to the race today. She had, as it turned out, eyes for only the horses. Perhaps if he had been one of the drivers in the race he might have proposed to her more successfully, shouting the words out as he drove by. She might have attended to him then. He should remember that for the next occasion.

The next occasion. There would be none with Lady Agatha. He had not actually ever gotten out the entire question this morning, although he had tried at least a dozen and a half times. Passionate? Her passions were so strong when it came to horses that a man could express an all-consuming, undying love for her and still she would not notice him if there were an equine body anywhere in the vicinity. In comparison, St. John felt rather cheated with only two legs to do him credit.

But he did not feel undying love for her, so it had never come to the test. Just a very strong admiration. Now, sitting in his dressing room, listening to his valet's advice on how to secure a bride, St. John was rather relieved Lady Agatha had not afforded him the chance to ask her to marry him. Perhaps she was not quite the appropriate match for him, after all. He enjoyed equine sport, indeed, but to make a lifetime's pursuit of it might have proved to be a bit wearying.

"A ring you say, Rogers?" he asked the man across the room from him. "What kind of ring do you mean? An heirloom?"

"Oh no, sir," the slightly rounded, nearsighted, balding man responded. Jeremiah Rogers had been successfully married for almost twenty years. St. John was all ears. "You haven't got one of those anyway, have you?" The valet straightened the cleaned waistcoat on its hanger and set it carefully back in the wardrobe, then reached over and put his hand on his master's evening coats. "Which one do you prefer for Lady Fitzwarren's dinner this evening, sir?"

"The blue. You're quite right. I haven't got one of those. When she died, Mother's jewels all went to my sister Amelia, and my stepmother wears only rings my father has given to her."

"You must go out and purchase a ring at the jeweler. Would you like some assistance, sir? I had some experience in that line when I was a mite younger, in the service of Viscount Dunworthy, you see." The valet stood holding St. John's deep blue superfine evening coat in one arm, a pristine, pressed white shirt in the other. St. John nodded.

"Yes, I should like your assistance, Rogers. And I thank you very much for offering it."

Rogers nodded smartly, then turned away so that Sir Pennworthy did not see the look of concern on the valet's face, nor the expression of compassion in the older man's eyes.

* * *

"Mademoiselle Pierce, I am so happy to finally make your acquaintance. I have heard much of your beauty and charm, but I see now you are more lovely than the reports suggest."

"Thank you, Monsieur Le Maine, you are too kind." Alethea curtsied and held her hand out to the Frenchman. Their hostess had just introduced them. He was of middling height, elegant form, and had extraordinarily fine features. His accent was almost nonexistent. He came on the excellent recommendations of both Ladies Fitzwarren and Fredericks, and he had just complimented her in a manner that any young lady would find head-turning. Additionally, Bertram Fenton was nowhere to be seen. The evening was almost perfect.

Now, if only Monsieur Le Maine would move a bit to the left so that she could take another good look across the room at the pale young lady sitting next to Sir Pennworthy.

Alethea caught herself up shortly, feeling a blush steal into her cheeks. Her lashes fluttered in confusion and she looked at the Frenchman quickly.

"Mademoiselle, you color charmingly. I am not sorry to have inspired it," Le Maine said in a pleasing tone.

Alethea scolded herself silently. As the Frenchman continued his flattery, she told herself that she merely sought an opportunity to thank the baronet. This evening was the first she had seen of him since that terrible afternoon in the Park, and having learned what he and his aunt had done for her, she felt indescribably grateful to him—*them*.

She had said as much to Lady Fitzwarren just moments ago as that lady led her across the room to meet Monsieur Le Maine, but the eccentric countess' response was enigmatic. "All in a good aunt's day's work," she had replied, then laughed merrily at what she apparently thought was a joke. Alethea took her words to mean that Sir Pennworthy was responsible for the generally accepted version of her escape from Bertram Fenton that day, and she wished to tender her thanks to him as soon as possible.

The occasion to do so did not come until much later that evening. After dinner in the drawing room, waiting for the gentlemen to finish their port and join the ladies, Alethea fretted about where best to station herself so that without appearing forward she could join Sir Pennworthy when he came in. She was at the edge of the room, vaguely attending to the conversation of two elder matrons with whom she stood, when the gentlemen finally entered and Alethea discovered that she need not have worried. Surprisingly, his eyes met hers straight off; seeing her somewhat hesitant gaze on him, Sir Pennworthy turned and came directly over to her.

"Miss Pierce, how are you feeling this evening?"

"Quite well, thank you, sir." Now that she had him before her, Alethea suddenly found it much more difficult to order her thoughts than she had imagined it would be. The man had, after all, proposed marriage to her not too many weeks earlier.

"I am glad to hear it." His eyes were quite blue and dark, and quite unwaveringly, unnervingly fixed on her. "My aunt's table was excellent this evening, was it not?"

Alethea blinked. Somehow the intent expression on his face had not prepared her for a comment concerning braised duck and curried sole to come forth from his lips. She looked at the lips in question, and then quickly away.

"Yes, sir, indeed. Quite excellent." Where had her tongue gone? Not her tongue—her wits!

"Her chef is an *émigré*, of course. Aunt Mellicent will have it no other way."

Alethea felt her nerves ease slightly. It was simply small talk. They did not know each other at all, really. Somehow, since the Park, she had come to imagine otherwise. She was a silly clunch! Still, she could not seem to find the words to come to the point.

"Miss Pierce, if I may be so churlish as to mention what must undoubtedly be an unpleasant subject for you—" His voice was low.

"Oh, yes, sir!" she breathed out in relief. "I am so very grateful for the assistance you and Lady Fitzwarren rendered me the other day in the Park. I cannot think what I should have done if your party had not been there at that particular moment to come to my aid."

She saw the self-effacing expression at once cross his handsome visage. He bowed.

"At your service, ma'am. My aunt played the greater part in assisting you, I believe."

"Oh, no, sir. You were very kind, and I am exceedingly grateful to you for your understanding. And yet more grateful for your putting it about that you did not come upon me by accident. I have been saved quite a deal of unpleasantness due to your actions on that matter, as well."

Sir Pennworthy's expression altered as she spoke. His fine mouth thinned to a line and his eyes, it seemed to Alethea, grew darker still.

"Are you yet free of—of unpleasantness, Miss Pierce?" he asked, his hard gaze searching hers. Under that gaze, Alethea suddenly felt as if she could not breathe, as if all of the emotions of the past four months were crashing down upon her at one moment. *Not here, dear Lord, not in the middle of Lady Fitzwarren's drawing room,* she begged silently, blinking rapidly to hold back the tears she felt gathering in her eyes and throat. With the greatest of efforts, she lifted her chin and swallowed.

"The situation is at present satisfactory." She clasped her hands tightly before her and willed herself to breathe normally. Nothing would come into her mind. She could think of nothing whatsoever to say. The unbidden tears crackled behind her eyes, threatening, and she watched as Sir Pennworthy nodded thoughtfully and then raised one brow.

"I noted the other day whilst strolling through Leicester Square a marked preponderance of chartreuse in ladies' bonnets this season, Miss Pierce. Do you think the fashion will take?"

Alethea stared in confusion at the baronet. Chartreuse? Ladies' bonnets? *Was* he a simpleton, after all? Then she watched in fascination as one corner of his mouth very barely creased before he spoke again.

"While not millinery adept, it seems to me a

rather odd color to put atop a lady's head, if anyone should ask."

Slowly, Alethea raised her gaze to meet his. Impossible. They thought him *dim-witted*? She took a deep breath, steadying herself, and swallowed.

"I myself," she finally replied, unshed tears retreating, "much prefer blue to yellow in my hatwear, Sir St. John."

Five

"Oh, Sir St. John! It is exquisite!"

The girl looked positively awestruck. But she had not said a word since he had produced the betrothal ring. Her mother, on the other hand, was in transports. St. John watched his future mother-in-law lift the gold and diamond ring out of her daughter's pale, yielding fingers and hold it up to the light of the morning sun wavering through the windows. She turned it this way and that, lowered her spectacles, breathed on it and rubbed it against the sleeve of her morning dress before gazing at it again in wonder. Finally, Mrs. Littler handed the ring back to her daughter and gestured for the girl to put it on. She presented St. John with a satisfied smile.

"You have made Penelope very happy, Sir St. John. Very happy indeed."

St. John lowered his gaze to the girl sitting across the tea table from him and gently took her beringed hand in his.

"I hope to make you happy for many years, Miss Littler."

The girl raised her eyes to him and he saw something like a ray of hope in them that warmed him. She was delicate, shy, uncomfortable around gentlemen. Not a bit of that excessive spirit that characterized some women. And she was most decidedly under the thumb of her mother; that was clearer than her crystal blue eyes and translucent skin. St. John felt an unexpected swell of gratification in knowing that in several weeks' time he would rescue this taking little thing from the overbearing influence of her mother. He could not imagine how this fragile girl had passed seventeen summers without entirely wilting away under the domineering hand of Mrs. Littler. St. John himself felt rather beaten down after only the mere fortnight he had spent in the woman's company whilst courting her daughter.

That would change once he and Miss Littler were wed. Devon was a long, long way from Cumbria, and St. John would see to it that if his delicate little bride did not wish to see her parents, she would not have to. Naturally, he would put up with Madam Littler if his wife wished to see her mother; but even those visits would have their limits.

"I am afraid I must be off now," he said and stood up, his betrothed and her mother rising to their feet as he did. "I am loath to leave, but I deeply regret that I have an unanticipated appointment with my man of business that cannot be missed." He smiled at Miss Littler, who returned his regard with a sweet curving of her pink lips and a lowering of her angelic lashes. Then he turned to the matron.

"Sir St. John, you are welcome at all times, for however long you should wish to stay," Mrs. Littler's smile was saccharine. "You shall be one of the family soon, after all."

St. John bowed.

"Madam, I am most anxious to meet with your husband when he arrives from the country. Please inform him that I should be happy to come here or to receive him in my own house on South Audley Street, whichever he prefers."

"Certainly, Sir St. John."

Mrs. Littler offered St. John her hand, and he bowed over it before taking his betrothed's light fingers and bringing them to his lips.

"Until tomorrow then, my dear." He was surprised at the slight trembling he felt in her touch, but her eyes showed no hint of fear, only demure maidenly reserve. He squeezed her fingers gently, and then followed the butler to the front door.

It was a rainy day in London, a rainy, damp, miserable, gray day. St. John strode down the puddle-strewn sidewalk as if the sun were shining brightly and he had everything in the world to be happy about.

He did. In three weeks' time, or a bit more, he would be married. He had put his ring of engagement—the ring that his valet had helped him choose at the jewelers two days before—on the girl's dainty finger, and she had accepted his proposal.

Accepted! St. John could barely contain his satisfaction. His chest felt full to overflowing. It was a remarkable feeling, this, imagining his own wedding—and marriage!—finally, after so many years. His bride-to-be was sweet and pretty in an angelically pale sort of way. She gave him the

impression with her gazes, which were more numerous than her words to him, that he was doing
her the veriest favor by bestowing his attentions
upon her. Taking little thing that she was, he
could not quite understand that, but was grateful
for the renewed confidence it gave him, nonetheless. Grateful, too, that his aunt had brought
her to his attention at her dinner party almost
two weeks ago.

He was, to be sure, a mite concerned at the
restraint Miss Littler typically displayed in conversation with him. But St. John felt somehow, after
having been in her company more than a half
dozen times, that there was more to her beneath
her timid exterior. Being ever in the presence of
her loquacious mother, Penelope had little opportunity to express herself fully, St. John imagined. As his wife, she would be free to say
anything and everything she wished, and at any
time she wished it.

His wife. He would have a wife. Outstanding!

His strides were light and long as they carried
him blithely through the drizzle westward toward
his house. So wrapped up in his comfortable
thoughts was he that when a passerby stopped in
front of him, he almost walked full into the fellow.

St. John barely pulled himself up in time to
avoid colliding with the gentleman. "I beg your
pardon!"

"Sir," the stranger said, looking at St. John
rather queerly. "There is a lady in a carriage
across yon street attempting to get your attention," he said shortly and not altogether approv-
ingly. "I thought you ought to know before more

people remarked it." Then he moved around St. John to walk away and St. John could have sworn he heard mumbled the words, "Young scatter-wit!"

He directed his glance to the halted carriage not twenty feet away and recognized the face of his youngest sister in the window. His smile, if possible, broadened.

"St. John!" Esther opened the door to the covered carriage as he approached it, heedless of traffic on the busy street. "We have been following you for two blocks and I have nearly shouted myself hoarse calling you! Have your wits gone begging?" She held out her hands and he grasped them and raised them both to his lips. Then he leaned forward and kissed her soundly on one rosy cheek.

She backed onto her seat and St. John climbed the step the footman let down and pulled himself into the carriage. He was met immediately with the enthusiastic embrace of his other half sister, and as he hugged her he greeted his Aunt Mellicent, whose carriage he had recognized from the street.

"Welcome to Town, ladies. Good afternoon, Aunt."

"What are you doing walking through the rain without an umbrella, Nephew? You will catch your death of a chill, foolish boy."

"Aunt Melli, you are unfair!" Miss Lilly Pennworthy exclaimed. "St. John is no longer a boy. He is a grown man, and you cannot scold him as you scold us so frequently."

"Hush, child! You are impertinent." A chuckle

rumbled somewhere beneath Lady Fitzwarren's yards of purple crepe.

"Silly, St. John may be a man, but men catch colds, too," Esther pointed out very correctly to her sister and then turned to her half brother. "But what *were* you doing walking down the street in the rain, St. John? You had such a peculiar look on your face."

Lifting Lilly's hand close to his face to examine the thin gold ring she wore on her smallest finger, St. John wrestled down the desire to tell the news he was longing to impart to his family. But he had not yet spoken to Miss Littler's father, and until he did, it was his and her business alone. And her mother's.

"I was taking a walk, scamp," he replied, lowering his sister's hand and giving it a squeeze before releasing it. "And what are you ladies doing tooling the streets of London on such a day?" He looked to his aunt, nestled in her corner of the carriage. St. John felt a peculiar prickling at the back of his neck as she regarded him steadily from across the small space. He shifted his gaze uncomfortably to his little sister.

"We are on our way home from visits," Esther replied. "Aunt Melli has been introducing us to all of her old friends—"

"Esther!"

"—and now we are going home to her house to see if anyone visited while we were out. We hope so," Esther added wisely, "because that means we are very sought after, if people cannot find us in when they have expected us to be in."

Still feeling the odd discomfort at the nape of

his neck, St. John glanced at Lilly, then back at Esther, and nodded soberly.

"I can see you have been learning the wily ways of Londontown quickly," he said. "Where is my stepmother today? Resting after the journey, I hope?"

"At our house, waiting for Papa to arrive. He is bringing the lemons with him, you see." Esther's voice was serious.

"Mama cannot leave the house without first applying her lemon mask," Lilly explained to him in a stage whisper, and St. John glanced to his aunt warily. She was chuckling once again, and St. John wondered if he had imagined the earlier expression he had glimpsed. The carriage was rather dim.

"Well, you are good to have stopped for me, but I do not wish to hold you up—"

"But we are here already, St. John," Lilly said, laughing fondly at her brother's error, and the door swung open for them to prove it. St. John climbed down and held out his hand to assist his sisters and aunt from the carriage.

"Will you come in and have a spot of tea and dry off, Nephew dear? You are a sight." The countess tapped his shoulder with her tiny red umbrella, and without waiting for his answer, strolled up the steps ahead of them all.

"I am afraid that I have an app—"

"Oh, do come in, St. John! We have been in Aunt Melli's company all morning and are certain she is fagged to death," Esther begged. "She has assured us that if visitors should come before nuncheon we will be on our own to entertain them. We are not yet quite sure how we would exactly go about that, this being London, and we suspect things are not done quite the same as back home in Devon. And of course, Aunt Melli *is* a countess."

St. John glanced skeptically up the stairs at his aunt's broad back, and then extended his arms for his sisters to take, one on either side of him.

"My man of business will simply have to wait."

They climbed the stairs behind Lady Fitzwarren, but when they entered through the open doorway, they did not find her alone. She was busy greeting several visitors who, having found her away from home despite an appointment to meet her there, had left their cards and were preparing to take themselves out again into the rainy day. Lady Fitzwarren apologized for their lateness. She made introductions, and when it came St. John's turn to bow he did so with nary an indication of the peculiar feeling that had returned to plague him—this time in his shoulders—when he set eyes upon Miss Pierce standing in his aunt's hall. They all adjourned into the parlor and Lady Fitzwarren rang for tea.

"I am so very glad you happened by today, Hecuba, for I have something I have been wishing to speak with you about for days now." Lady Fitzwarren had settled herself comfortably by the tea table, and requested that Lady Fredericks's younger daughter, Elizabeth, pour out for them. "But first, you have brought with you the most charming Monsieur Le Maine. How are you, my dear man? Our dreary London weather is not too much of a shock for you after the sunny shores of Italy? I understand Florence was *quite* beautiful this past winter."

"Ah, *ma belle* Florence! How I miss the sun and music and *gaieté* of the Italian peasants!"

That was all of the commentary on Mediterranean culture St. John heard before he turned his attention fully to the girl sitting in the chair beside him.

"I am happy to meet your mother and your friend, Miss Pierce. Have you and Miss Wisterly made many visits already this morning?"

Alethea opened her mouth to reply, but closed it again when Sir Pennworthy continued.

"I have never quite understood why we refer to the middle of the afternoon hours as the morning here in London." He turned his eyes back on her. "I beg your pardon, Miss Pierce, but it has long confounded me."

Alethea found herself smiling, and she strove to control the amusement that bubbled up in her at the baronet's most sincerely expressed comment.

"I cannot say, sir," she replied with admirable equanimity. "But perhaps it has something to do with the weather. So often it seems to be dim and the clouds cover the sky more usually than not, so that the sun is barely visible. Perhaps Londoners do not recognize afternoon when it begins because they have no indication it has arrived."

"But what of clocks? Surely London homes have clocks in them. Why, I have a solid clock in mine, and would be willing to provide a clock for anyone who might be lacking one but who perhaps cannot find the funds for it."

Alethea could not tell if he was roasting her, or if he was as entirely sincere as he sounded.

Then she chanced to glance to his side, and the grin on his young sister's face gave her the answer.

"You are very generous, sir," she stated securely. "But I would not wish you to spend your fortune on that. Instead I shall write a petition and send it to Parliament, calling for the installation of clocks on all street corners and vendors' shops. That should serve the purpose, don't you think?"

Alethea was smiling, sharing her pleasure with Lilly Pennworthy over her brother's shoulder. When her eyes met the gentleman's again, she was surprised by the familiarly intent look in them as he regarded her.

"Quite."

"St. John! Tell us when you are going to take us to Astley's Amphitheater and to the Tower to see the menagerie!" Esther had scooted her chair close to her brother's side and now placed an entreating hand on his arm. Alethea watched as he put his own hand on top of his sister's for a moment, and a sharp sensation caught in her chest.

"When your mother tells you I may, imp," he replied affectionately.

"You must stop calling me 'imp,' St. John. I am a Real Lady now, and you must treat me as one. As you treat Miss Pierce. Am I not correct?"

"Correct, indeed, imp." He turned his blue gaze on Alethea again and she became aware that she must have been staring at him, so surprised was she by his direct regard.

"Miss Pierce, will you join me in a drive in the park with my sisters tomorrow, if the weather is fine? I am certain they would benefit from the example of a Real Lady to show them how to get along with the more beneficial Town entertainments."

His smile, so breathtakingly handsome, was also so sweet that Alethea forgot everything else and accepted the invitation without hesitation. A half hour later as the ladies departed Lady Fitzwarren's house with Monsieur Le Maine in tow, Alethea recalled too late that she had promised the next day to the Frenchman. He wished to take her to see an auction of a Tuscan master at Christie's, and until this afternoon she had been perfectly pleased to accompany him. Chewing on her bonnet ribbon on the way home in the carriage, and thinking over the delightful half hour she had just spent talking with Sir Pennworthy and his sisters, she did not know whether she should solve the mix-up by following her breeding or her inclination.

Breeding won. St. John received her carefully worded note of apology that evening as he was dressing to go out to his club for dinner. Setting it down on his nightstand with unwonted care, he drew the ruined cravat from around his neck and crumpled the starched fabric in his hand.

It was not until an hour later, ensconced in a chair at Brooks's and partaking of an excellent meal in the company of several friends, that he realized it was the sheerest good luck that Miss Pierce had declined his offer for the following day. He had no business driving out with that young lady, neither tomorrow nor any day in the future, he thought, stunned. He was betrothed.

Six

St. John was summoned to the home of his
affianced lady at the unfashionably early hour of
eleven o'clock the next morning. Having already
ridden in the Park, bathed and breakfasted, he
found no fault with this unusual request, and
presented himself in the drawing room at Thirty-
one Portman Square on the hour. He found his
bride-to-be alone in the room, and recognized
instantly that this was the first time he had ever
been truly alone with her, a fact that must have,
he was certain, portentous overtones. He stepped
forward and took her delicate hand in his.

"Your servant, ma'am," he greeted her, bowing over her hand and kissing it lightly. He was
astonished to have it jerked away from him
abruptly.

"Oh, Sir St. John, you mustn't! I cannot—! You
cannot know—!" She pressed her hand to her
breast in distress.

"What is it I cannot know, Miss Littler?" St.
John replied without alarm, although the fact
that his betrothed had just uttered more words
to him in one outburst than he usually wrested

from her in a whole morning's conversation did register in his intelligence.

"Mama—You see, Papa—! How can I say—?"

St. John took the girl's slender hands again and drew her down to the seat next to him.

"Miss Littler, has your father arrived from the country so soon?" Unaccountably, St. John felt his spirits weaken. It was not that he was afraid of this unknown fellow, only that speaking to Mr. Littler would be the finalization of all he had wished for for so many years. It made a man feel rather faint . . . with joy, St. John supposed.

"He *has* arrived," she managed in a weak voice, "and he has brought *such* news with him." She paused. "I am betrothed!"

St. John barely heard the faintly uttered words. Brow compressed, he leaned forward to understand her better, and Miss Littler promptly sprang up from the sofa and away from him. Slowly, he turned his head toward her to find her standing near the empty hearth. He noted, to no purpose, how remarkably quickly the frail young girl had moved.

"Perhaps, my dear, you could repeat for me the news your father has brought with him from Cumbria," he said. "I do not believe I heard you perfectly."

Her eyes widened, but not in fear or dismay. St. John could almost wager she was excited.

"I am betrothed." This time her voice was a bit stronger than he remembered having heard it before. Her words, however much they should have comforted him, rather failed to, given the unambiguous placing of them in the conversational context.

"I rather expect you mean to say that you are betrothed to *another*, Miss Littler?"

Her jaw seemed to set as he regarded her, her pink lower lip protruding beneath its partner in a surprisingly unappealing manner.

"To another, Sir St. John!" she repeated, hands still clasped tightly against the white fabric of her bodice. She was quite pale, delicate blue veins showing through the fair skin of her hands and forehead as she stared at him. "To Lord Appleby, if you must know. He is not nearly so wealthy as you are, but Mama says it is much better because he is not in Trade. And he is an earl and has two estates in Yorkshire."

"How very impressive," St. John murmured and stood up. He had not meant to remain sitting while the lady stood. His mind must have gone wandering. Inexplicably, St. John felt his heart beating strongly.

"Your father arranged this engagement for you while he was in the country?"

"They signed the contract yesterday. Mama and I had not known they would—" she stopped herself suddenly, mouth open, and looked about her as if seeking something or someone. She looked like a rabbit caught in the midst of dogs. St. John had for an instant the strangest idea that he was at the moment perceived to be some sort of predator. He straightened his shoulders.

"I am—"

"Mama said I must not give it back!" she cried, moving another pace away from him. "She says that a gentleman never expects a lady to return a gift of jewelry, unless it is an heirloom, and this is not one, so I do not have to give it back to you."

The girl's death-grip on the ribbons of her high-necked gown—and not incidentally the fingers of her left hand—suddenly made perfect sense to St. John.

"Naturally, Miss Littler. I am happy you should have the ring, although regret that it can no longer signify what it was once meant to." He bowed deeply. "I shall take my leave of you now, madam. Please extend my congratulations to your mother and father on the anticipated enviable disposition of their daughter in marriage. Your servant, ma'am."

It was extraordinary how rapidly St. John found his heart to be beating when he stood again on the street in front of the Littlers' town house. The sky had opened up overnight, and the sun was now shining with radiant brilliance onto the clean-washed brick of the sidewalk. A warm breeze, fragrant of new spring blossoms, drifted from the direction of the green nearby, and birds chirped with merciless good humor from every treetop along the street.

There ought to have been more drama to it. St. John took a deep breath, steadying himself, and began walking slowly down the sidewalk. There was something terribly dissatisfying about breaking off one's engagement in such a brief, dispassionate manner. Perhaps he should have ranted, raved, broken something? There were a good number of fine porcelain figurines in the Littlers's parlor. He was certain he could have put his hand on one quickly enough to have suited the purpose. But then he would have had to replace it. Terribly inconvenient if the cast had been destroyed already, or lost. He had dabbled only once in porcelain manufacturing. Too much trouble and too many talented, well-entrenched competitors to make it worthwhile. Glass was safer.

St. John put his hands into his pockets. He looked thoughtfully down at the tips of his high-shine boots as they moved rhythmically out in front of him, one after the other, carrying him up the empty street.

Seven

"Two estates in Yorkshire! Is that what she said?"

"Mm. Something like that. D'you know the fellow?"

"Appleby? Slightly. Paunchy, fifty if he's a day, but the worst thing about him," Lord Bramfield paused to make his point dramatically. "His breath. Positively rank, morning and evening. Never been next to him without wanting to gag, my word as a gentleman."

St. John Pennworthy was conversing with his friend Timothy Ramsay, Viscount Bramfield, recently returned from his wedding trip in Italy. They stood together at the edge of the ballroom holding up a set of twin Ionic-style columns which were, in their turn, not holding anything up, as they were purely decorative and their capitals only reached as high as the taffeta canopy hanging from the ceiling. The Baron and Baroness Mowbray had outdone themselves on behalf of their twin daughters' Come Out. It seemed as if the entire *beau monde* was packed into the Mowbrays' ornate albeit spacious town house, and most of the guests were in the ball-room, at that.

St. John's mouth formed into a slight *moue* of distaste and the viscount laughed.

"I don't suppose you mentioned to her *your* properties, did you? No, I didn't think so." He smiled broadly. "You are better off without her, my friend, and that is the happy truth," Lord Bramfield said, clapping St. John on the shoulder and laughing again. "Don't know what all the rush is, anyway. A man needs to find the *right* bride, I tell you, for marriage otherwise is a pen-ance any clear-headed fellow should avoid like a plague."

If his friend's tone were not so jovial, and so mixed with obvious affection for the young lady his gaze was even now following across the floor as she walked toward them arm in arm with an-other young lady, St. John would have wondered how blissful *were* the first months of Lord and Lady Bramfield's wedded bliss. Ramsay's talk was all bluster, though; that was obvious. The man was as happy as could be with his new viscount-ess, and it was clear on his face as he looked at her now. St. John bowed when Lady Bramfield and Miss Wisterly approached and greeted the gentlemen with smiles.

"St. John, it is the greatest pleasure to see you again." Cassandra Ramsay extended her hand to shake St. John's warmly.

"Marriage has made you yet more radiant than you were already, my lady, if that is possible." He was sincere. He should have complimented his friend Timothy equally sincerely if the other man would not have coshed him right then and there for the flattery. But Timothy and Lady Bramfield did indeed both look quite gorgeously happy.

"I would wager, Sir St. John, it was not *marriage* that brightened my friend's visage, but *meeting* Lord Bramfield in the first place." Miss Belinda Wisterly looked wisely at him, and St. John nodded thoughtfully.

"It was something of a miracle, it's true," Cassandra Ramsay said softly, and somewhat shyly. "I had not thought I could be so certain upon just once glance." She looked to her husband, but he had become engaged in conversation with the others in their group. The comment only reached the ears of Sir Pennworthy and Miss Wisterly.

"It seems magical, does it not?" the young bride's friend said affectionately, unembarrassed at the intimacy of their conversation.

St. John was not uneasy either. It must indeed be wonderful when one felt so certain one had found the right mate. Reflecting on this, his gaze drifted to the dance floor, skimming the couples engaged in the set, and then wandered across the clusters of people standing all about the room. Then it came back to rest on Miss Wisterly. He opened his mouth, and then shut it.

"—said it was impossible to travel before May because of the rain," Lady Bramfield was saying when he thought to attend to his companions' conversation again. "But we encountered no such problems, happily, on our journey."

"Pray forgive me, Lady Bramfield, Miss Wisterly," St. John interrupted deferentially. "I believe—I think I may be needed right now." He gestured slightly with his champagne glass toward the back of the ballroom, taking in at least three hundred people with the movement. His step-mother and elder sister were visible among the crowd. "If you will excuse me."

St. John made a slight bow and smoothly drew away from his friends. Moving around the edge of the ballroom, he glanced to the side once to note that his stepmother and Amelia had moved further into the crowd. He had seen them to be on the verge of doing so before he had used them as an excuse to leave his friends so abruptly. Then, without further ado, he slipped out of the ballroom and into the corridor lead-ing to the Mowbrays' private chambers.

It had been at least three weeks since Alethea had last set eyes on Bertram Fenton, and she was pleased to be able to acknowledge to herself that there were occasionally days when she did not think of him even once. His features were be-coming hazy in her memory, and if she closed her eyes she could not even remember anymore the color of his favorite waistcoat.

Green.

He had told her that the evening of the Twelfth Night play at the Bridgewaters' Christmas house party, just after he had told her how beau-tiful she looked in her emerald velvet ball gown.

Spanish coin. He had been flattering her and making advances toward Sylvia Sinclaire for the duration of the entire holiday, Alethea was now certain. They were two of a kind, Miss Sinclaire and Mr. Fenton, and they were welcome to each other.

It was just proving rather more difficult to exorcise him as entirely from her heart and mind than Alethea had hoped. It did not help that he had sent her yet another bouquet of roses the previous day. Yellow, a color as ambiguous as the note attached. She had refused to look at the note, but Octavia had read it aloud anyway:

> *Time may pass, time may tell, but you shall always be the most beautiful lady of my acquaintance, and the only one in my heart.*

What on earth was that supposed to mean? That she would become an old maid without him, or that he was growing old waiting for her to change her mind? The man was a sad rattle, she was beginning to see, and an atrocious poet.

But this evening, sitting with her mother and Mrs. Pierce's friends at the edge of the Mowbrays' dance floor, resting from the last energetic country dance she had engaged in, Alethea had let her guard down. Suddenly there had appeared before her two thickly muscled legs in pristine white trousers, and as her gaze traveled up past gold waistcoat and black superfine, her heart had sunk. Finally she had raised her eyes and met the smoldering gaze of Bertram Fenton. Alethea sighed.

It had been impossible to cut him, sitting trapped as she was in a corner and under the interested gaze of not only her mother's friends but several other nearby matrons. Too strong a reaction to him would put the lie to the idea she had tried to convey in public that he meant nothing at all to her—for good or for bad. She had not, however, accepted his request for a dance. When, after several minutes during which she had responded to his questions with monosyllabic answers, he finally yielded and went away. Then Alethea had hurried into the crowd to find refuge with her own friends.

There he had found her again, but how he had managed since then to sequester her in a corner of the Mowbrays' surprisingly dim breakfast parlor Alethea was not at all certain. She thought it might have something to do with the way he had maneuvered her into the corridor to the ladies' retiring room with promises to obey her desire to leave her be if only she would give him one more chance to plead his case. His eloquent lips had entreated for her mercy; his hands had taken hers between them and carried them to those lips so gently that Alethea had not quite noticed until a moment later that somehow he had led her away from the retiring room door. She was being led into the entryway of another, much darker and entirely deserted room instead.

Cursing herself for a distracted fool, and for allowing her head to be turned again—and so brazenly!—by one who had used her so poorly, she stood inside the doorway of the little parlor and pulled her hands away from his at last, insisting that he escort her back to the ballroom at once. Truth be told, his mawing was making her stomach ill. Although his soulful eyes and gorgeous mouth beckoned, listening to him felt to Alethea something like looking upon chocolate bonbons when one had the headache: nauseating, in a perverse way.

"This is not at all acceptable, sir. Please do step aside and allow me to return to my party," Alethea now said in a firm voice, seeing that the gentleman was standing directly in her way; if she were going to depart, she would have to push past him anyway. She put her hand to her mouth and clutched her reticule in her other.

"I feel terribly unwell and am quite afraid I will be ill if you insist upon keeping me here any longer."

"You are unwell, Miss Pierce?" His tone was so concerned Alethea almost thought it did not sound like him at all. His eyes were like a beautiful dog's, wide and brown. "Please do let me help you to recover yourself. Perhaps a little fresh air will relieve you."

Swallowing hard on her rising gorge, Alethea found herself being led rather firmly against her will across the small room to the window. "I am quite fine, sir," she said, plucking ineffectively at his grip on her arm as he reached out and opened the latch of a window, pushing the pane open for some air. "If you could simply see me back to my mother, I would—"

His lips descended upon hers so quickly that Alethea did not even have time to breathe before she was trapped under the onslaught. Dropping her reticule, she pushed frantically at his shoulders, but it was like pushing at a brick wall. His arms went like a vise around her. She moved her head sharply to the side, disengaging her mouth for a moment.

"Mr. Fenton! Take yourself off me this very inst—" He covered her mouth again and she struggled in his tight grasp more desperately.

"Darling Alethea!" His words were blurred between heavy kisses. "Why will you not speak to me? All I want is to be able to talk to you, to—"

"It does not seem as if that is exactly *all* you want of the lady, sir. And it appears to me that the lady does not share your wishes."

The voice came from the open doorway across the room. Feeling her captor loosen his grip in surprise, Alethea freed herself and sprang away instantly, pulling a sleeve back onto her shoulder that had been tugged away from its rightful place. Then she looked from her attacker to her rescuer, and her heart sank. Her hand went to her mouth again, and this time she truly did feel as if she might be ill. The man next to her spoke abruptly.

"What is this all about, man? The lady and I were having a private conversation which you have very rudely interrupted!"

"Indeed?" Sir Pennworthy's voice was soft, in marked contrast to the other man's blustering anger. She watched as the baronet's gaze slid to her and then away again, his expression unreadable.

Alethea felt her throat constrict and tears suddenly gather behind her eyes. But she refused to let them come forth.

"Mr. Fenton has mistaken himself, Sir St. John," she managed to say with admirable control. "We have had something of a misunderstanding, he and I, but I am certain he would have come to understand me shortly. However, I am very grateful to you for stepping in to clear things up more quickly. Thank you." She squared her shoulders and finally raised her gaze to meet the baronet's. He was standing very tall and still in the partially opened doorway, the gaze he trained on her rather too knowing.

It was unbearable. Biting on her lip, Alethea moved quickly across the room, brushed past Sir Pennworthy, and went out the parlor door.

She was unable to escape the ball. Her mother would not take her hints, and in fact since she did not really have the headache she claimed, Alethea thought it unfair to deprive her parents of the enjoyment of such a fine party. In a way, Alethea was glad of it. She could not run away and cower at home forever. Bertram Fenton would undoubtedly come looking for her again. And in any case, it had been terribly uncomfortable having to wait for over a week to thank Sir Pennworthy for the last time he had rescued her; this way she could express her gratitude immediately and get it over with. If only she could find him again in this crush!

His lips had not felt at all the way she remembered them. Bertram's, of course. Alethea stood next to her friend Belinda in a group of several others, not really attending to the conversation around her; she tried to recall how it had felt to kiss Bertram Fenton at Christmas time.

He had kissed her twice then: once searching for the Yule log, innocently under the mistletoe while their friends looked on, and again in a stolen moment during the Twelfth Night party, less innocently. She supposed he might have thought tonight that he had the right of precedent, seeing that she had once been more than happy to share her kisses with him in the shadows whilst music played on in the other room.

Alethea sighed. What was it that she had felt for that roguish, overgrown puppy-dog in the first place? The man did not seem to have an ounce of honor in him. Unlike some *other* gentlemen of her acquaintance.

She was shaken out of her reverie by the sound of Lord Bramfield's raised voice, and she lifted her gaze to meet the subject of her musings.

"There you are, Pennworthy. We were just beginning to wonder what had happened to you. Did your mother and sister coerce you into dancing with a fourth cousin you did not know existed before this evening, old man?"

"Timothy, you must not roast him so," Lord Bramfield's wife said fondly, turning her gaze on the man who had just approached their group. "St. John has probably been very properly occupied, as you ought to be as well, instead of standing here teasing everyone who passes by." Cassandra Ramsay was smiling upon her lord.

The viscount's eyes beamed as he bowed over his wife's hand.

"Milady, may I escort you into the dance, a most proper activity, I believe?"

She tapped his bent head with her fan and giggled.

"Yes, you may, milord!"

Alethea took advantage of the moment of diversion provided by the newlyweds to raise her glance to Sir Pennworthy. He was looking at her without hindrance as Lady Bramfield moved away from between them, a slight, pleasant smile on his face. His ballroom expression, no doubt,

Alethea thought. Nevertheless, she felt her stomach tighten.

"Miss Pierce, may I have the pleasure of this dance?" He might have already extended his arm to her, for all they both knew she would say yes. But he had not.

"I would be delighted, kind sir." Then he did raise his arm, she placed her hand on it, and he led her into the set.

There was little opportunity to speak during the ensuing minutes, the movements of the country dance being particularly active. But when it was over, Alethea was winded enough to honestly warrant a moment on the other side of the open terrace doors. When Sir Pennworthy suggested it, she gladly agreed. They strolled toward the doors and out onto the lantern-lit terrace. She took a deep breath of fresh night air and turned to face him.

"Sir, it seems I am again in your debt," Alethea stated, but not too loudly. There were other couples taking the air on the terrace as well, though none close by. "Thank you for the assistance you rendered me. I was in a rather—ah—uncomfortable situation. I am very glad it was you who happened upon it. I hope I do not presume too much in feeling confident that I can trust you to keep this unfortunate incident private."

Her words halted her. How humiliating that this man had witnessed what he had! And what was she to him to presume upon his loyalty? Suddenly, she knew not where to look.

"I am sorry to know you were discommoded this evening, Miss Pierce. Again, I am at your service." He sketched a slight bow and Alethea felt, if anything, more uncomfortable hearing his reasonable tone and unremarkable comment.

"I did not intend—What I mean to say is that it was not my desire—my *wish* to—My father does not—" she stammered. For once he did not step in and assist in easing her verbal confusion. Instead he regarded her with his dark blue eyes, his hands clasped behind his back.

"The timing of your arrival—," she began again and then stopped herself once more. The timing of his arrival? Just what *had* Sir Pennworthy been doing walking into that parlor at that particular moment, in the area of the house not in public use for the ball? Alethea's eyes narrowed but his expression did not alter.

"Sir, I do not mean to question your activities, for indeed they are none of my business and certainly you have been a great help to me this evening," she said before her courage deserted her. "But if I may ask nonetheless, what happened to bring you into the room at just that hour this evening?"

Sir Pennworthy regarded her steadily.

"I felt I might be needed," he replied.

And that was that. What could she possibly find to say in response to such a statement?

"Oh. I see. Well. Thank you."

Alethea turned to face the nighttime garden. Not two feet away from her on the balustrade, inconspicuous in a dark shadow, lay her discarded reticule. Feeling warmth fill her cheeks, she reached over and pulled it to her silently.

"I am persuaded that we design our gardens with such care in London so that we will not forget the beauties of the countryside whilst we are here," the man beside her said thoughtfully. "The city holds so much fascination that it would be easy to forget how much we love the rest of England. What say you to my idea, Miss Pierce?"

Alethea sighed quietly, feeling the strange, unpredictable presence of the man beside her with surprising comfort given the evening's events. *Event.*

"I should never forget the serenity of the country, Sir St. John, were I to spend a thousand nights in London without a garden in sight."

"I suspect you carry your garden within you, Miss Pierce."

Alethea's head turned at the words, and she opened her mouth to respond, but closed it again just as quickly. The baronet was gazing out sightlessly into the silvery-dark night.

And I suspect, Sir St. John, Alethea considered to herself as she looked at him thoughtfully, *that perhaps you speak more of yourself than of me.*

Eight

Three days later, St. John took up Miss Pierce, Miss Octavia Pierce, and the Misses Lilly and Esther Pennworthy in his open carriage for a morning drive in Hyde Park. The hour being unfashionably early, they had the road nearly to themselves with the exception of a lone horseman or two, or an occasional party of strollers along the way. They were having a famous time of it. The schoolroom misses had taken to each other at first meeting and immediately busied themselves with vociferously comparing their by-now vast knowledge of London—as if volume could make up for actual experience—and with teasing the Pennworthys' doting old groom quite mercilessly.

Up on the box with Sir Pennworthy, Alethea was enjoying herself completely. While occasionally unpredictable, the gentleman's conversation was all that was agreeable. It did not signify in the least that she had, minutes earlier when he handed her onto the seat, colored up extraordinarily quickly in response to his rather simple compliment on her appearance. It was not every day a lady was told she reminded a gentleman of cherry preserves.

Alethea was content. She felt very becoming indeed in her new cherry-red walking dress and matching pelisse. The white feather on her red-trimmed cadet's-cap bonnet made her appear quite dashing, too, she had thought when looking into the glass this morning before Sir Pennworthy's arrival. Octavia had caviled at the time it had taken Alethea to dress; she wanted her sister to study their father's new atlas with her instead of "primping and preening" in front of her mirror, all for a silly drive in the Park. Alethea had laughed, telling herself that she was simply in a frame of mind to take extra especial care with her toilette today.

She hoped he *liked* cherry preserves.

St. John adored them.

He had not meant to say exactly that to Miss Pierce, but occasionally the words coming out of his mouth were not what were in his head to begin with. She had not seemed discomposed by the compliment, however wide her eyes had for an instant grown. But he had become accustomed to that already. The two were at present speaking on general topics when the girls sitting in the carriage behind them commandeered their attention.

"St. John, I have told Miss Octavia Pierce twice now that you have been to India, but she simply will not believe me," Esther said from the backward seat, twisting herself around to face her brother. "Tell her yourself or we shall never have an end to it."

"Is it true, Sir St. John? Have you been to

Deepest, Darkest India?'' Octavia said rather breathlessly for a girl who despised the cultivation of die-away airs in maidens.

"I believe those adjectives are usually used to describe Africa, Sister," Alethea said on a chuckle, sharing a grin with Lilly Pennworthy as she glanced back.

"Indeed. India is more usually spoken of as Exotic rather than Deep and Dark," St. John replied without a hint of color in his voice. Spying his mouth, quirked at the corners as he continued to look forward, Alethea was certain he quizzed. "In fact I have been there, once, several years ago, Miss Octavia."

"Was it quite, quite fascinating? What took you there, Sir St. John?"

Octavia had only yesterday been poring over the map of India in the atlas. Alethea found herself peculiarly interested in Sir Pennworthy's journey, uncomfortable as she was with her sister's innocent questioning of his motives for making it. The conversation was approaching too close to that topic normally not discussed between ladies and gentlemen of so little acquaintance: Trade.

"It is a land of colors, sounds, sights, and smells that are hard to imagine, Miss Octavia, so unlike England it is," he replied. "They eat food so hot a man is barely able to breathe after tasting one mouthful. They wear turbans around their heads and they go barefoot in the public streets. They use elephants and camels for everyday chores we would not even consign to a mule. And they are a people more multifaced than the English, Scotch, Irish, and Welsh all put together."

He had turned slightly in his seat to see the girl's eyes shining with pleasure at the description. Alethea quite unaccountably felt the breath go out of her as she stared at his profile so few inches away. Her gaze traveled down past his crisp white cravat and across the blue kerseymere encasing his broad shoulders, beyond which she saw the riders. She gasped involuntarily.

St. John shifted his gaze immediately to Alethea's face and then turned to see what had occasioned her sudden arrest. He straightened his shoulders and looked forward.

"I traveled to India on business, Miss Octavia, intending to stay for only a short while. But the country was so magnificent I did not leave until almost two years later." His tone was bland, but even so Alethea could not believe he did not recognize the man on horseback that with his two companions was about to pass them on the road.

"Two years! When was that, Sir St. John?" Octavia asked curiously, mentally tabulating how old one needed to be to travel to Exotic India.

"When he was barely older than Lilly, is that not right, St. John?" Esther offered proudly.

It was all Alethea could do not to stare at the approaching riders. They were certainly staring at her. Or not at her, actually; at Sir Pennworthy. How extraordinary.

"I was twenty-one at the time. Quite a few years our sister's elder, Esther." Alethea thought perhaps he glanced at her for a moment, but as her gaze was now in her lap, she was not certain.

"That was after Oxford," Esther said. "St. John was at Magdalen, you know, Miss Octavia."

"Oh, please call me Tavy. It's what everyone calls me."

"And you shall call me Lilly, please. Esther, do stop bragging about St. John. It is not polite."

The horsemen were almost abreast of the carriage. Alethea looked beyond her companion's profile—that which had given her pause only a moment before—and at the face of Bertram Fenton. He was no longer looking into their carriage, giving them the cut direct, although his two companions were still staring—rather, glaring—at Sir Pennworthy. But Alethea spared not a moment for their noxious gaze. Her eyes were glued to the red, purple, and black bruises which Mr. Fenton sported in great profusion beneath the brim of his fashionable hat. His left eye and split lip were swollen, as well; she now noted that his right arm was tucked underneath his jacket in something of a sling, it seemed.

Alethea's eyes widened in amazement. Then the riders passed; she turned her head and set her unseeing gaze to the path ahead of them.

"Lilly! Did you see that man's face? It was awful! All beat up, as if he had been in some kind of carriage accident or something."

"Hush, Esther! You will give Tavy and Miss Pierce a disgust of you carrying on in such a fashion!"

A carriage accident *was* in fact the story the man had put about, St. John had learned the previous evening at his club. All for the better. But how she could care so for a man who would blame such bruises on innocent horses, he could not fathom. The fellow was not only a libertine, he was a cad.

Alethea was reflecting silently. Bertram Fenton was not quite so handsome with a purpled face, for certain. She had gone a long way in reassessing her attraction to him even before she had caught sight of his mangled visage just now. His continued defiance of her clearly stated wishes regarding their connection had cast a considerable pall over her appreciation of his sensuous good looks. More unattractive was the idea that he had somehow gotten himself into the condition in which she had just seen him. Carriage accident, indeed! Alethea had spent enough summers among Belinda's and Cassandra's brothers to know what a human hand could do to a human face if sufficiently provoked. What could Mr. Fenton have possibly done to inspire such ferocity on the part of another man?

As she considered this not unexpected addition to Bertram Fenton's list of unappealing character traits, Alethea's gaze traveled distractedly to the ears of the matched pair in front of them, up the harnesses, and to the gentleman's Hessians propped neatly on the boot rest next to her own feet.

The baronet's understated elegance was something like Bertram's, she considered, although he tended to exude less raw virility than the dark-haired man. Perhaps it was simply Sir Pennworthy's character that suggested that, she determined as her gaze continued to travel the lengths of his muscular legs to the gloved hand resting on one knee. He was so very unassuming, and that little bit of eccentrism that others attributed to dim-wittedness went a long way to distracting one from his otherwise very masculine attributes, if truth be told. Why, a man who could drive a pair with one hand as Sir Pennworthy had been doing for most of this morning could not be said to lack the talent and strength of the most enviable of gentlemen.

As Alethea listened with half an ear to the conversation her sister and the Misses Pennworthy were animatedly engaged in behind her, she felt a tingling nervousness all of the sudden scamper through her veins. He was a very enigmatic man, this man she was sitting beside right now. . . .

What a silly pea-goose she was! Alethea chided herself. She had been so wrapped up in Bertram Fenton's albeit understandably head-turning obsession with her that she had entirely failed to think why she felt so *peculiar* in Sir Pennworthy's presence. Perhaps, too, the baronet's gentle manner and quiet humor had distracted her from what she had until very recently not recognized constituted a man's true masculinity. Gaze fixed on his resting hand, she realized that in fact her unsteady nerves with him on several occasions, including this very moment, could be attributed to nothing more than the fact that she was, in the end, simply quite attracted to him!

A brace of birds erupted suddenly from a shrub at the edge of the path, causing the horses to skitter nervously. Alethea dazedly followed Sir Pennworthy's gloved hand to his other as he took the reins in both and calmed the team with a sure touch. Then her eye caught the flash of a corner of white gauze peeking out underneath the edge of the glove before he flexed his wrist gingerly and then laid it again on his knee. Alethea turned her gaze to Sir Pennworthy's face.

"Sir, have you hurt your hand? I could not help but notice that it is bandaged, and you have been favoring it this morning, I think," she said. "I do hope that you have not felt obligated to drive us today when perhaps you should not?"

"Oh, do not worry a bit about it, Miss Pierce," the elder of Sir Pennworthy's two half sisters said from behind. "He told us he split the skin at Gentleman Jackson's Salon yesterday when he missed his opponent and hit the boxing cage instead." Lilly and Octavia broke into giggles, and Alethea thought she heard Esther Pennworthy state that it was what men deserved for taking up such silly pursuits in the first place.

But she was not attending. Very slowly Alethea's gaze traveled from the gloved hand on Sir Pennworthy's knee to the gentleman's face, his expression entirely immobile as he stared ahead at the roadway. Her eyes narrowed. There was a redness, albeit a very slight one, around the edge of the baronet's left eye.

It could not be. Alethea swallowed.

"Sir," she began deliberately and very quietly, her voice not carrying to the giggling girls behind, "might your injury instead have been caused in a *carriage accident,* by chance?"

St. John turned his gaze on her, brows rising haughtily over sapphire eyes.

"Madam, I take umbrage at your inference. What manner of cow-handed clod do you imagine me to be?"

The question went unanswered. His presumption on her behalf was preposterous, improper, and had gained him a ruined hand and a bruised eye in the bargain. Nevertheless, responding to the barest glint in his otherwise non-committal eyes, Alethea felt her lips curve into a slow smile of certainty. A moment later she almost forgot she was supposed to be feeling grateful, and not awestruck, when her companion responded with a satisfied smile of his own.

St. John had not given up his search for a wife. Quite the contrary: being in almost constant company of late with the blissful Lord and Lady Bramfield kept the longing rather more powerfully at hand than ever. But he found himself otherwise busily occupied as the spring progressed, with business engagements and also with activities devised by his stepmother and sisters for which he, more knowledgeable about London than his father, was obliged to act as guide. Lilly and Esther having taken to Miss Octavia Pierce strongly, that young lady was more often than not invited to accompany them. So it was that St. John frequently found himself in company with not only his family, but with both Miss Octavia Pierce and Miss Pierce, and Miss Wisterly as well. Lord and Lady Bramfield made a comfortable addition to the group on many occasions, and not a few temperate late April and early May days passed with them all together exploring the life-like characters at Madame Tussaud's Wax Museum, the marvels at the Tower, the wildlife wonders of Lord Geoffrey's new menagerie, the paths and vistas of Richmond Park.

The pleasant company of Miss Wisterly did not go unappreciated by St. John on these outings. She was an agreeable companion: interesting, curious, and levelheaded enough to attract any man who had recently suffered from the various inconsistencies of damsels of another sort of temper. He found it inconvenient and not a little irksome, to be sure, when on occasion she regarded him with something very much like bewilderment, but those moments passed quickly enough.

Nevertheless, it was not this infrequent discomfiture that prohibited St. John from considering Miss Wisterly in the light of a potential bride. It was the fact of her relationship to the recipient of his first proposal that closed the door firmly on that possibility. Miss Pierce and Miss Wisterly were bosom bows; it was unthinkable to St. John that were Miss Wisterly to look favorably upon an offer from him, he should have to spend the rest of his days anticipating and simultaneously dreading visits from his wife's friend.

But that was not to be thought of. *She* had refused him already. Even if she had not, St. John had—understandably—determined not to tarry with women who had other gentlemanly prospects at hand.

Mr. Bertram Fenton was not much of a gentleman, as far as St. John was concerned, but he was undoubtedly still at hand. Miss Pierce had been pleased, he was certain, with how he had seen fit to deal with that blackguard's latest insult to her person. But her satisfaction at knowing Fenton well castigated for his misconduct did not mean he was not still firmly embedded in her affections. St. John had known individuals to behave in more contrary manners. His own distraction when in the company of Miss Pierce was proof positive of the obstinacy of human nature.

Thus it was that late one evening at cards with some friends in one of the more discreet and reputable gaming establishments in town, St. John reflected quite deliberately on the hints cast his way by a beautiful young widow with whom he had for some years been acquainted.

It was generally known that Mrs. Hinde, having two years ago emerged from mourning an elderly husband and in the meantime having taken full advantage of her newly found freedoms, was now looking for a more permanent companion. Attendant this evening more out of a desire to escape his own empty house than anything else, and a bit blue-deviled in the bargain, St. John was not aware of the lady's interest until Mrs. Hinde paused behind him in moving from one table to another and placed her hand gently on his shoulder. Looking with mild surprise from the bejeweled fingers to his companions at the table, it became clear to St. John that the speculative glances they had been leveling at him for some minutes did not in fact mean that his game was particularly excellent this evening.

"I see, Sir St. John, that you are losing tonight," Mrs. Hinde said softly close to his ear as his table-mates pretended unsuccessfully to look elsewhere than into her low-cut bodice. St. John felt the warmth of her breath on his cheek, took in her fragrant rose scent, and glanced down at the paucity of chips at his place.

"Perhaps if you were to play the right card," she murmured, "you would find yourself lucky, instead." Her fingers trailed away down his arm as she moved off. St. John shuffled the deck in his hands. He dealt, not looking at his companions, and started the play.

It was more than two full minutes later that he realized nothing had passed at the table after he turned over the first card. He looked up, surprised to find three pairs of eyes leering at him above three smirking mouths. St. John looked down at the center of the table. The Queen of Hearts lay flat on her back, staring up at him.

Nine

He was clearly not the only man who could not keep his eyes from her this evening.

St. John had arrived tonight in the same party as Miss Pierce, but was now standing across the room from where she and Cassandra Ramsay were engaged in conversation with Cassandra's younger sister, Elizabeth, as well as Lady Fredericks and their hostess. The concert would begin shortly, and although their party had been separated when they entered the Wentworths' home, he along with Timothy Ramsay and Horace Fredericks would rejoin the ladies to listen to the music.

St. John could not wait, although enjoying the sight of Miss Pierce from across the room was quite satisfying enough in its own right. Until moments ago he had been conversing with several gentlemen of his acquaintance, but his gaze kept straying back to her. He had excused himself from the conversation, too distracted to attend his companions well.

Something about her tonight—her glittering eyes, rich hair, shimmering gown?—was different. Or could it be that just that afternoon when they were taking ices together at Gunters with their sisters she had smiled at him just *so*, and he still felt warm from the look? He knew not. It seemed, however, that his was not the only male attention captured by her beauty this evening. It became clear that the gentleman standing behind St. John was was referring to Miss Pierce when his companion spoke her name. Eavesdropping, St. John only heard the conversation already in progress.

"Delectable legs. And she has had her skirts dampened, I am certain of it," he heard a masculine voice state confidently.

"You are mistaken, March," another man said. "Miss Pierce is quite captivating in the gown, I agree, but the girl does not need to succumb to such devices to show off her figure to advantage. A mail sack would do the job, I imagine." The man chuckled, but not lasciviously. Nonetheless, St. John's mouth hardened. He reached up to tug gently with two fingers at his cravat. The room had become rather warm suddenly.

The Viscount March, crudely as he had expressed himself, did have the right of it, however. The gown the young lady in question wore tonight was fashioned of a silver-shot gossamer silk that flattered her lithe figure magnificently. St. John had found he could not even consider the fabric critically, so distracted was he by how lovely it looked on the lady wearing it. Absurd for a man of business. But just this once he would forgive himself his lack of application. This once.

"Do you know much of her, Gilford?" The

drawl behind him was affectedly lazy, but clearly interested.

"Only what others have said. I've had a dance or two with her," the other replied. "She is very light on her feet."

Reasonable, tactful. Gilford was an army captain, St. John recalled. Always politic, those officers. The other man was not.

"She must be a prime goer if Fenton is interested in her—a spirited romp in the saddle, I'll wager. From what he says, she is besotted with him. But I have a mind to show that cocksure fellow a thing or two." The other man's voice had taken on a decided bravado. "I plan to have a go at her tonight, if I find the opportunity."

The noncommittal snort from the captain signaled the topic was closed, and St. John was gratified that at least both of the men were not thorough rogues. He raised his wineglass to his lips and sipped thoughtfully.

It passed through St. John's mind a few moments later that a new, thick Aubusson carpet was just the thing to decorate one's home with. It was too bad Mrs. Wentworth's was now stained in one spot a lovely claret red. Of course she could always move one of the marble busts she seemed to have all over the room on top of the place. Just the perfect size, really, to cover the spill. A pity, too, for Lord March's elegant buff pantaloons and embroidered waistcoat.

"By God—!" The man was sputtering.

St. John looked up from his suddenly empty glass.

"Terribly sorry, March, old chap!" he said, eyes ingenuously wide. "Demmed rug jumped up and grabbed my shoe, of all things. Perfectly dreadful. Exceedingly embarrassed, I say." A footman walked by, and St. John set his glass on the silver tray.

Lord March's face was white. St. John shook his head in sympathy.

"I shall send my man around to you tomorrow morning first thing to take care of the bill. Most humble apologies," he said, bowing. As he turned and strode away he was certain he heard the peer behind him mutter the words, "Clumsy dolt."

As St. John approached the other members of his party, guests were beginning to make their way toward the rows of chairs set up in the middle of the spacious room. The Wentworths were known to host some of the finest concert evenings in London; the chairs in their music room were unequaled in an elegance that matched the quality of the music, if not famous for their comfort. But for the first time ever at one of the Wentworth musicales, St. John did not even notice the seating. It was taking all the concentration he had not to stare at those beautiful legs of which he had not needed the viscount March to tell him to notice. The girl's skirts were modestly dry, but he wondered if Miss Pierce knew just how marvelously flattering the cut and fabric of her gown were.

Alethea did have some idea that she looked particularly attractive that evening. She had seen it in the glass in her room after she had dressed, and she had seen it in Horace Fredericks's eyes when he had arrived earlier in the evening to escort her to his mother's house for dinner. As

Horace was a very old acquaintance, almost like a brother to her, Alethea was not accustomed to such appreciative glances or such sincere compliments from him. And here she had thought she was blessedly free from the sort of attentions Monsieur Le Maine gave her for at least one evening!

It was no time before Horace had resumed his usual familiar manner, but in the carriage on the way to the Frederickses' residence Alethea had yet felt a tremor of nervous expectation. She had in fact dressed very carefully this evening, instructing her abigail to prepare the new gown for her to wear and helping the girl to arrange her hair so that it fell in shining cascades from a twisted knot down her nearly bared back. The front of the gown was all that was modest and appropriate for a young lady, but the feel of her hair on the skin of her back felt delicious and very daring—as the exclusive French modiste had intended. The thin, textured silk of her gown swaying against her legs likewise felt marvelously bold.

By the time they had arrived at the Frederickses' house Alethea was nearly trembling with anticipation. The evening was warm, and she had only the light shawl she had carried in her hand. Preceding Horace through the drawing room door, she had made an effort not to search the room for any one particular member of the party. She had greeted her host and hostess, and then her gaze met Cassandra's. Her friend had grasped her hands and told her how beautiful she looked, and when Alethea looked to the viscount Bramfield his bright blue eyes were alight with certain appreciation. Then with a breath she had turned her regard to the man standing beside Lord Bramfield, the only other person in the room save seventeen-year-old Elizabeth Fredericks.

Nothing.

Sir Pennworthy, leaning casually against the mantel, bent forward to bow. He wished her a good evening; but his dark eyes showed not only a lack of appreciation of her carefully manipulated perfection of appearance, but even perhaps a tiny little flicker of . . . *ennui?* Alethea had never, she was sure, seen him look *less* interested in anything than he had right then. The evening's tingling excitement had crumbled like so much dust inside of her.

It served her right, Alethea thought, for caring so much what a *man* thought of her—again.

Perhaps it would have been more accurate to say St. John had never been *more* interested in a lady's appearance than at the very moment Miss Pierce had walked into the room that evening. Unless one counted the present moment. As he had struggled to do so in the Frederickses' drawing room earlier, St. John now schooled his features into a mask of gentlemanly reserve and stepped up to offer his arm to Miss Pierce. Perhaps if she were right next to him he would be prohibited from staring at her like a slavering dog. She placed her hand on his arm.

No—that was not going to work. He could feel the light touch of her fingers like fire through his coat sleeve as they moved toward the rows of chairs, smell the redolence of summer lavender emanating from her hair and skin. The room really was dreadfully warm.

"Here will do quite well, sir," St. John heard her say and released her to her seat with what could not be enough speed. He sat down beside her and, from his other side, Timothy handed him a *libretto* for the performance. When St. John turned back to the young woman to his right, she was studying hers with furrowed brow.

"How foolish I have been to forget my reading spectacles," she said with a rueful twist of her lips and turned her regard to him.

St. John raised his eyes to hers guiltily. He could not possibly have been staring at the one long curl of chestnut hair that was resting so delicately on the edge of her bodice, where fabric met flesh. His breeding was much superior to that.

"Indeed, ma'am, I wish I had a pair I could offer you at this moment," he managed rather nicely, he thought, all things considered. "May I instead offer to read the text to you out loud?"

Alethea's cheeks were warm. His look had been rather blank, for sure, but it had been rather pointedly directed below her chin, nonetheless. But the diffidence was still there in his face, the same disinterest from earlier in his eyes. He had simply been woolgathering, she decided, not knowing where it was he had fixed his gaze. The idea was very lowering.

"You are kind to suggest it, but I shall not saddle you with such a chore," she replied with what she hoped sounded like good nature.

"It would rather be a pleasure, madam, to assist you in any endeavor." His voice was warm.

Alethea opened her mouth to respond, but lost her words quite suddenly as the sapphire eyes before her seemed to wink to life again under her own gaze. She realized after a moment that she was sitting with her mouth open, entirely silent.

"Ah—uh—"

"I was under the impression, Miss Pierce," the baronet said unremarkably after several undirected syllables had issued forth from her mouth, "that ladies did not relish admitting the use of such items as spectacles, if I may be so bold as to observe it."

Alethea thought to close her mouth.

"I have never understood what could be so wrong with spectacles to produce such animosity in the hearts of women," the baronet continued when she did not reply, "for I would think they should be treated as treasures for what they do for a person's appreciation of the world around her, or alternatively the literature in front of her." He assessed her for an extended moment. "You have admitted to the use of them, and for that I am in great admiration of you."

For *that*.

Alethea finally found her voice again, and her wits.

"Thank you, sir," she said. "I am indeed grateful for the help my spectacles render me, and would not consider disparaging them. I cannot fathom what those who eschew wearing them are thinking about to defeat themselves, all on account of senseless vanity. I am ashamed, in fact, that I thought not to bring mine tonight, when I knew perfectly well I should want to read the *libretto*. I do not know what I could have been thinking of to be such a ninny-hammer." Then a dimple appeared in her cheek, and her lips curled in humor as she looked at him sideways. "And since I have had them made so very particularly, ridiculously delicate and unobtrusive for evenings such as this, I am especially thwarted."

St. John felt himself smiling, and raised one brow.

"Miss Pierce," he murmured, "do you mean to say that *senseless vanity* has played its part in your unimpaired appreciation of the world?"

He watched her peek at him from under lowered lashes, suppressing her own grin.

"I fear so," she admitted in a low, laughing voice. She sighed lightly. "But the spectacles would have matched this particular gown so very nicely, you see."

St. John sat back in his seat, noticing that the pianist had just taken his place at the instrument to begin the concert.

"I cannot imagine, madam," he whispered as the crowd quieted, his dark and surprisingly tender gaze on hers, "that it would be possible for even the most priceless ornament to enhance your beauty yet more tonight."

For the next many minutes, Alethea did not know if the singer before them was a tenor or a soprano, or an entire choir, for that matter. On the other hand, beside her and much too painfully aware of at least *one* thing for his own good, St. John was struggling quite manfully to concentrate as well as possible on the performance of the talented singer. He noted the excellent qual-

ity of the soprano's voice, the extraordinary skill
with which she enunciated each mellifluous note,
each pathos-laden word, so that together lyrics
and music filled the room with a sound that
made a man tremble to hear its transcendent,
golden magnificence. Or perhaps that trembling
was caused by something more close at hand. He
could not be certain.

It was at least twenty minutes before St. John
trusted himself again to glance at the young
woman next to him. She was sitting upright at
the edge of her chair, attention fully directed to
the performer at the front of the room. Her
hands were clasped in her lap and her posture
was very straight, the fall of dark red-brown hair
down her back luxuriant in its wavy richness. A
man could lose himself in that gorgeous hair,
lose himself drawing it aside to touch the
smooth, bared skin of her back beneath.

St. John put his hands into his pockets. He
looked around him. Where was the damned fire
blazing in this room?

His gaze wandered as he sought to steady his
nerves and passed over the figure of Captain Gilford, now bereft of his former companion.

Men like March were a plague, St. John mused
grimly. And Fenton. It amazed St. John to think
a sensible girl could lend her affections to such
a rogue. But it was true. From what he had
heard—if rumor were to be credited—she loved
the knave still.

Not, of course, that this meant anything at all
to St. John. Miss Pierce was beautiful. She had a
charming, light sense of humor and was almost
entirely unselfconscious and not at all vain. She

had an interest in a great many things, including sailing, wax production, unusual flora and fauna, beekeeping and honey making, not to mention drawing all of the above—all of which he had learned about her over the course of the past weeks of entertainments spent in her company. But none of that signified in the least. If she admired Fenton, despite his ill-mannered behavior toward her, then so be it.

So be it, indeed, St. John castigated himself as he directed his attention back to the soprano who seemed to be drawing to the finale of her performance. It truly did *not* signify in the least to whom she gave her affections. He raised his hands to applaud when the performance came to an end, joining in the appreciative lauds the singer received from the assembled guests. He was glad to have her friendship, of course. A lady such as Miss Pierce was a pleasure to be in company with. A gentleman was just *that* because he could happily claim the friendship of such a woman and not expect anything more of her. Furthermore, he was feeling rather glad now that he had made plans to join several of his friends later that night at an elegant gaming house. There he was bound to meet a certain lovely widow whose interests were most definitely *not* otherwise engaged.

St. John was congratulating himself on his righteous self-interest as the applause petered out and the young woman beside him turned to him.

"That was beautifully done, was it not, Sir St. John?"

Her eyes were unusually bright, her color high, touching cheeks and brow with a hue that brought her expressive features to even greater light. Her lips were parted slightly in an exhilarated smile and a hand rose to her collarbone to register the swelling breath that she took in sheer satisfaction.

"She has the most magnificent voice, does she not? And the song was wonderful. Simply wonderful!" she said with feeling.

St. John feared he stared.

"Miss Pierce, you are weeping."

She reached up in astonishment to feel the wetness on her cheek, and her eloquent hazel eyes widened.

"Why, so I am!" she said in surprise. Then she reached out her other hand and set it on his arm for the briefest of moments. "Is it not marvelous?" Her smile was one of unadorned delight.

Faced with this extraordinary vision, St. John found himself completely speechless.

Several hours later, the cool night air caressing his face as he slowly walked the dark steps up to his front door, St. John could still feel the place where she had touched him as if it were a brand on his skin. When his footman opened the door for him and the baronet moved silently into the candle-lit hall studying his sleeve as if it were about to speak to him, the servant said nothing at all. Pomley especially did not mention the half-foxed young gentlemen who had called on the baronet hours earlier, expecting to have been met to go out with them tonight. Sometimes, the footman had learned from experience, it was best to make these decisions oneself for one's unusual employer. Instead, he simply closed and bolted the door behind his master and, when Sir Pennworthy had climbed the stairs to his rooms, put out the light.

Removing her gown before bed in her own room that night, Alethea regarded the silken dress without really seeing it. It was so odd . . . she mused, braiding her hair deftly and tying it with a ribbon. She climbed into her canopied bed. One look from a man sometimes revealed so very much—at least of what was in one's own heart, if not his.

She had not known until Sir Pennworthy had complimented her so sincerely and looked at her so intently in the Wentworths' music room that she did not love *Bertram Fenton* anymore. The sudden, out-of-the-blue, clear-as-crystal realization had caused her so much unexpected relief at the moment it came that she had wanted to laugh out loud—for being so fickle or perhaps so wise, she knew not, truly. Then her ear had caught the soprano's song and it had almost seemed to Alethea as if that woman was singing for *her,* expressing so perfectly with her strong, honeyed voice the strange and unexpected sensation of freedom Alethea felt more and more strongly as each moment passed. The music had soared, and Alethea's spirits had gone along with it. When it was over, she had turned quite impulsively to the one person who, for some reason, she felt could entirely understand.

One look, indeed, revealed so very much sometimes. Especially when the eyes doing the looking were a warm dark blue, and the lips through which no words were being uttered were the most alluring Alethea had ever seen in her life.

She had experienced the second great relief of her evening when Timothy Ramsay had suddenly clapped his friend on the back and the long thread of silence between her and the baronet had been broken. For Alethea now had the strangest certainty that if she had stared one more moment at the man, and if he had been anyone other than the Superlative Gentleman St. John Pennworthy, she would have kissed him— right there, in the middle of the room, surrounded as they were by their friends and several dozen other members of the *ton*. The surprise she felt, however, was not at her certainty at her own desire, but at the inclination she had from the unmistakable intent in his gaze that he would have fully welcomed her advance.

Ten

Light catapulted into the dark sky, breaking into a thousand tiny starbursts and trailing in bright, spindly lines downward to peter out and disappear in midflight. Alethea gazed up at the fireworks exploding in the night sky and mused that sometimes she herself felt quite like one of those Chinese rockets.

Around her, Vauxhall Gardens teemed with festive activity. In addition to the fireworks which had just commenced, paper lanterns hung from trees throughout the pavilions and tree-lined walkways, illumining diners, strollers, dancers, and the orchestra arranged under a canopy on the lawn, filling the air with music. That air was rather warm, and Alethea cooled herself with her ivory-handled fan as she looked about her at the people wandering by Lady Fredericks's box. Monsieur Le Maine sat at her side, solicitously transferring a wafer-thin slice of ham from his plate to hers, Alethea having just noted how much she enjoyed the portion she had been served.

She smiled and thanked him, and wondered how she would ever manage to eat it. It was as if Monsieur Le Maine was trying to fatten her up for something, she could not wonder what. Only that morning he had sent her a box of white-chocolate-covered rose petals, of all things. The day before he had insisted upon ices at Gunters. Two evenings earlier at a ball he had loaded her plate with lobster patties and trifle until she had had to carry it with two hands to the supper table. She supposed a gentleman exiled from his own country could be affected in his brain in some way from the shock, but if so, this was a very peculiar way of manifesting it.

Lady Fredericks placed her serviette on the table and stood up, drawing her guests' attention.

"I believe it is time for a stroll. Horace?" She held out her hand to her son, and he stood and offered her his arm. Lady and Lord Bramfield stood as well, and the rest of the party arranged themselves in pairs as they exited the box. Alethea took the arm of the Frenchman, as everyone seemed to expect her to do these days. This was despite the fact that she would have been just as happy on Horace's arm or with the escort of any other of the gentlemen, young or old, in their party tonight. She was becoming irritated with the general assumption of her set that she welcomed the Frenchman's company more than that of any others. He was all that was charming, but she was not in a mood to be charmed these days. She had had quite enough of charm lately.

Alethea laughed ruefully at her private musings as they strolled out under the starlit night. Monsieur Le Maine bent his curly head to share in her joke.

"Ah, mademoiselle, you have the laughter of

a Naiad, the spirit of a Sea Nymph, and the voice of a Muse."

Alethea smiled demurely. She had become inured to the man's flattery weeks ago, although she was recalling a great deal about ancient mythology in the meantime and so did not discourage his foolishness. She did not know if she could if she tried, to be sure.

"Mademoiselle, what is it that has you downcast this evening?" he said suddenly, in the midst of a string of compliments, and Alethea turned to look at him. "You cannot hide it from me. Your face is like that of Persephone: when it is in the sun all the earth is alive and I am warmed; but when it is in shade I feel the cold of winter and I shiver."

"I am quite well, monsieur. Thank you for your concern, but you have mistaken me, perhaps."

In fact he mistook nothing. Alethea had come out this evening full of the excited anticipation of experiencing Vauxhall for the first time; during her Season the previous year she had not had the opportunity. The lights, the food, the magical music, the crowds of people mingling together under the stars—all had delighted her for the first hour they had spent strolling and then dining in the Gardens. Then she had seen them.

Several boxes away, three elegant gentlemen and three exquisitely dressed ladies shared a box beside a charming fountain adorned with a waterfall around whose cascade floated a half dozen lily white swans. Looking at the diners beside the fountain, one instantly saw that they were an intimate group, well known to each other and none of them neophytes of this par-

ticular slightly *risqué* venue. Of course Vauxhall
was an entirely acceptable entertainment, if one
attended with one's *mother*, or aunt or some
other appropriate chaperone. That these ladies
were obviously free of such inconvenient con-
straints Alethea understood all too well for her
tender years. All three of the ladies were young,
but one of them Alethea knew to be already
widowed, and another was a lady whose marriage was notoriously one of convenience in the
very strictest sense. Of the gentlemen, two were
unknown to her, and the third was the baronet
St. John Pennworthy.

Recalling now how during supper he had
leaned toward the petite brunette next to him
and bent his golden head over her sleek, dark
coiffure, how the two had laughed together at
what he had said, made Alethea's stomach feel
quite as if she had had one too many bites of
ham after all. Lady Fredericks's suggestion of a
stroll had been a welcome relief from the strain
of trying to not look over at the other party every
few seconds. But at least sitting in the box she
could see where they were and what they were
doing. Here, wandering along the midnight
paths of the garden—a garden full of winding,
promising alleys and dark, intriguing shadows—
Alethea could only imagine. She had an excellent imagination.

Why it should matter what St. John Pennworthy did with his evenings—and nights—was
an irksome question to Alethea. She was fond of
him, as her sister Octavia was, and she had of
course come to recognize that she was very attracted to him. What girl of her acquaintance was

not? She had *not*—emphatically—formed any sort of a *tendre* for him, however; that was indisputable. Her foolish fancy of the night of the Wentworth musicale signified nothing whatsoever. Firstly, she had surely imagined his look. And secondly, she had not seen him since then, in several days in fact, and she felt perfectly fine about it. That was proof enough of her indifference.

In any case, men were tiresome trouble, Alethea reminded herself. Sir Pennworthy was no exception, especially given how he was this evening demonstrating himself to be little better than Bertram Fenton—in one area of his life at least. They were all the same.

One of them nudged her out of her reverie when he released her arm and put his hands gently on her upper arms.

"Mademoiselle Pierce, would you be so kind as to stand for a moment, just here, just by this flowering shrub—what do you call it? Lilac, *non?*" Monsieur Le Maine had halted himself and Alethea on a pathway along the edge of a high hedge. The bush next to which he was asking her to stand bore flowers that were wilting in the warm night air, as Alethea felt she must be doing as well. She set her mouth and her look questioned the Frenchman as she felt rather than saw the rest of their party move away slowly down the path. He let go of her arms and stood back a pace from her.

"*Magnifique!* You are she! You, and this Lilac, together you are my painting!" His tone was awed.

"I beg your pardon?" Alethea's brow curved into a skeptical frown.

"I shall paint you like this, *mon amour.* I shall paint you just as you are, you shall be my model, *ma Muse.*" His voice was hushed as he misused his myths, and Alethea realized that the sounds of the festivities seemed to come from quite a distance away.

"Monsieur, I do not understand you well, but I should like to continue along with our friends, if you do not mind," she said, trying to sound patient but feeling rather the opposite. Perhaps London was getting to her finally. Perhaps it was time to go home to the country and socialize with normal, only half-insane people again. Pure, humble country folk. Preferably only women.

"But, mademoiselle, it is you!" her companion exclaimed. "You have wrenched from me the artist that I always knew was buried deep within me. Now I am free to create!" The Frenchman moved toward her again and took her hands in his gently, wonderingly. "I wish to paint you, like this—but not yet."

Alethea looked over her shoulder. Their party had disappeared entirely around a bend in the hedge. "Not yet?" She turned back to him.

"Not yet, *mon amour.* First you shall eat. My Aphrodite must be as rounded and overflowing with love as Raphael's! And then," he said in a low voice, moving closer, "you shall come to my studio where I paint, and I shall feed you grapes peeled delicately by my own fingers, and your skin shall glow in the morning sunlight through the windows, and we shall make love—"

"Monsieur! You forget yourself!" Alethea, who

had forgotten *herself* for a moment in the combined irritation and amusement of listening to him, balked.

"You will see how beautiful it can be, *mon amour,*" the Frenchman murmured fiercely, grasping her shoulders and drawing her against him. Pulling back, Alethea raised her hand and struck him forcefully on the cheek. He released her immediately and put his hand to his face, a shocked and wounded expression crossing his handsome Gallic features.

"Mademoiselle? *Ma chère?* What have I said? What have I done?" His voice was bewildered.

Alethea stared at him in amazement.

"What have you done? What *haven't* you done?" she cried. "What haven't you and the sorry lot you call men done to insult and badger and inconvenience women who would not give you the time of day if they were not born and bred ladies in the first place?" Her voice had risen, and she was barely aware that Monsieur Le Maine backed away from her a step and then another. "Why, you have done just about everything you can possibly have done to give me a disgust of you and your whole sex, that is what! And you are entirely unaware of it, which is the most astonishing element! You have flattered me and cajoled me and importuned me and made copious apologies and promises to me which you have not kept, and you have lavished your attentions upon me without ever once wondering how it might make me feel to see you enthusiastically engaged in charming another, very beautiful woman who cannot possibly be as warm as I am right now given that she is wearing her *shift* as a gown tonight!" She was shouting. "What have you *done?*"

There was a sudden silence into which Alethea's last words fell, hung on the air, and then fizzled. She blinked, and Monsieur Le Maine was standing before her, his face a mask of confusion and contrition both.

"But you are the most beautiful woman I know, mademoiselle," he said rather pathetically. "I do not understand."

Alethea's eyes widened and then, abruptly, she began to laugh, laughing until tears came into her eyes and she had to put out her hand to the Frenchman's shoulder to steady herself. When she was finished and her mirth had entirely passed, she dried her eyes with a scrap of lace and turned toward the path where their friends had disappeared.

"Come along, monsieur," she said, "It is high time we caught up with the others."

"La, St. John! I do not recall you being this clever when Edmund was alive!"

"I was not. I have only just discovered wit this evening, Rosalind."

They were walking along a dimly lit path of Vauxhall Gardens, Mrs. Hinde's hand tucked securely against St. John's ribs, her half-exposed bosom pressed rather closely to his arm as a consequence. St. John looked down at her upturned face, more than pleased with the glistening red of her parted lips as she smiled knowingly at him.

"And does this discovery have anything to do

with me, darling St. John?" the widow asked with a pretty lift of one finely sculpted brow. Her thick lashes fluttered. "Have you perhaps saved up all of your cleverest quips and most amusing witticisms simply in order to divert an old, lonely friend from the cares of the world resting so heavily on her frail shoulders?" She sighed eloquently.

Quips and witticisms were not exactly what the baronet had felt an uncomfortable surfeit of since the Wentworths' concert. St. John drew his seductive companion to a halt under a tree that sparkled with silvery-pink blossoms in the midnight darkness. He brought her gloved hands to his lips with slow assurance.

"You are hardly old, my dear Rosalind." He kissed the fingers on her left hand. "Hardly careworn." His lips caressed those of her right, one after the other. He moved his hands to her bare arms. "And your shoulders are too delightful to mention without putting them to good use."

He bent his head and kissed the smooth skin of one bared shoulder and felt her shiver as he moved his lips along her neck.

"St. John, I always thought that you were not interested," he heard her say as his hands moved down her arms and came to rest at her narrow, uncorsetted waist. The fabric of her gown was tissue thin.

"You were married," he murmured into the dark, silken hair behind her ear. She sighed.

"Edmund has been gone these two years already, and I out of mourning for a twelvemonth," she whispered, arching her neck to welcome his kisses. "Why have you not said something before this?"

His hands slipped up her waist, thumbs caressing the lower curve of her breasts as her fingers gripped his arms.

"Why hurry a good thing, Rosalind." It was a statement rather than a question, and as his hand shifted and she moaned, their lips finally met. St. John pulled her against him, hands moving against her back, and he kissed her gently at first and then more forcefully as the embrace deepened. She felt remarkable in his arms, curved and soft, a fragrance of roses on her skin denying the gentler aroma of the apple tree's blossoms above them. She clung to him with flattering enthusiasm, enthusiasm that was driving his temperature quite dangerously high. He could feel every inch of her petite but very womanly body pressed against him, feel her lips underneath his, her hands clasping at his shoulders. She drew away from him for a moment, breathing heavily, and St. John enjoyed the vision of her heaving bosom.

"You are delicious, St. John," she said breathlessly. "I had heard that the young ladies' knees turn to water when you smile at them. But how their insides should turn to jelly were they to have you thus."

St. John drew her to him again into another long, hot kiss, series of kisses, and her hands went up to his face, fingers running through the short golden locks behind his ears as she met his kisses with an increasing fervency of her own. He slid one hand around behind her, shifting his hips against hers, and she moaned again.

"Rosalind," he said, mouth against hers, "I cannot wait."

"No—no—I, too, do not want to wait, darling." Her lips devoured his. His pulse raced. Her breath was coming quickly.

"I can arrange"—he felt her hand move between them—"for a special license"—and she touched him—"to be married—"

"To be *what*?"

All motion had stopped. With effort, St. John opened his eyes and found himself staring into the exemplar image of shock and dismay. For those were the emotions painted clearly on Rosalind Hinde's exquisite face. He was speechless.

"Married?" she said in amazement, drawing away from him. "St. John, whatever made you believe that I wanted to marry you?"

The words hit him like little daggers—to his loins rather more than his heart, it was true. Daggers, nonetheless.

"Please do not misunderstand me, darling St. John," she said with more control now, regaining her breath. One hand rose to play at his collar as her eyes tarried there, then she raised her gaze to his. She had regained her equanimity again, speedily. "I do adore your company, and you are by far the most gorgeously appetizing man of my acquaintance—"

St. John bowed slightly.

"But I have no wish whatsoever to be married again. Not ever!"

He looked at her with veiled consternation, desire dissolving on the warm night breeze.

"Then what meant you by the numerous subtle suggestions about finding a more permanent companion that were directed my way in the past week?" he asked, not entirely as evenly as he would have liked.

"Darling! I want you to be my *paramour*, not my *husband!*" Her tone showed her amazement at his slowness. St. John gently removed her hand from his collar and straightened his cravat.

"I had understood that it was preferable for the two to be one in the same."

She snorted elegantly. "If you are rather old-fashioned," she said, not unkindly, and then her eyes narrowed slightly. She stood for a moment thus, regarding him with humor and, St. John cringed to recognize, pity.

"Your point is taken, madam," he said flatly.

"I do not suppose," she said, hesitating a moment and then continuing, "that you would be willing to revise your ideas of *companionship* to accommodate me, would you, St. John?"

He looked at her for a long moment, and then shook his head.

"No, my dear Rosalind. However tempting the suggestion, I fear I am not the man you are looking for."

The beautiful widow sighed and then took a deep breath. She reached out and slid one finger along his cheek and jawbone.

"Delicious," she said on a sigh, one brow raised. "Some young lady is going to be very lucky some day, that is truth."

St. John raised his gaze to the pink-flowered tree glowing softly in the moonlight above them, and was silent.

Eleven

St. John did not leave his house for a full week. He spent the days working on business arrangements, writing letters, and taking cold baths. Several cold baths.

Sex was overrated. Passion was blinding, and it was a damned nuisance, as well. It obscured what truly mattered—a man's heart. At least St. John thought that if he were still to possess such an item after the spring he had come through, passion had certainly done its part in obscuring it lately.

The days were growing longer and warmer and London was beginning to lose its interest as the *ton* deserted the humid, busy city for the country. Thus when St. John emerged from his self-imposed seclusion, he found several of his set already gone, and remembered the notes that had come around to his house during the past week that he had not answered. Served him right. One note had only arrived that morning, however, and St. John made his way to Lady Fitzwarren's home without concern that he would find the windows shuttered and the knocker gone when he arrived.

"I am fond of Harriet, you understand, but she

is terribly trying sometimes, with her crotchets and aches and pains and constant groaning. The woman physicks herself every ten minutes, at least!" Lady Fitzwarren was sitting in her breakfast parlor, the remains of an excellent repast spread around her. St. John chewed slowly on a hot crumpet he had buttered, and regarded his aunt blandly. "It is why I called for your escort today, St. John. I simply could not *bear* going there by myself."

"Craven, madam?" he said laconically.

"I am frail, weak when it comes to generosity and patience, a human like any other," she responded with only a tiny flare of drama. It was, after all, not yet noon.

"Not *any* other, Aunt," St. John's mouth quirked up at one edge. "What of Esther and Lilly? Has the sheen of visiting dulled for them, and they still so young?"

The countess brushed crumbs off her bosom and lap with a lace-edged serviette. "Why, it was they who suggested I engage you, Nephew," she said casually. "You see, living with Harriet is a lady of great intelligence and learning whom Lilly believed you would find interesting."

St. John's brows did not so much as twitch.

"And how would she have gotten such a notion into her head, madam? I do not recall having mentioned that I was friendless of late."

"No," Lady Fitzwarren replied, wiping her fingers one at a time on her napkin, and sipping her coffee before she continued. "But she thought that perhaps if you were still on the lookout for a friend of—shall we say?—a *particu-*

lar sort, you might look to Miss Gretehed for, mmm, inspiration.''

St. John looked intently at his aunt. Her pin-point black eyes glinted merrily as they met his gaze from across the table. St. John sat back in his chair.

"Amelia told you."

Mellicent Fitzwarren put her hand to a small silver box on the table next to her, opened the etched lid, and drew forth a pinch of snuff. Her inhalation was followed by a sneeze.

"I cannot think what you mean, child. Your sister is the soul of discretion.''

St. John snorted. Then he sat thinking a moment.

"She believes I err."

The countess shrugged diffidently. In the morning her conversation was invariably less lively than after dinner. Her convictions aged as the day did.

"My niece is a sweet thing, and none too shabby in the brainbox, to boot. You ought to heed her, St. John."

"And so I have." He thought of his elder sister's advice and of Felicia Strapley, of Rogers and Miss Littler's fantastically expensive ring. Obviously it was his half sister's turn, now.

"I shall be happy to accompany you to Lady Juno's residence this afternoon, ma'am," he said finally, reaching for another crumpet.

"Famous," his aunt said shortly but rather more heartily than he had expected. *Revision: his half sister and aunt's turn.* St. John could hardly wait for the experiment to begin.

* * *

She was angry with him.

Not the tall, smooth-haired, serene-countenanced woman on the settle beside him. Miss Gretehed seemed, in fact, to be perfectly content that he was attending with interest to her every word, which mostly concerned the health, humors, and moods of her employer, who sat with his aunt across the Chippendale tea table from them.

St. John had not yet been able to make out the signs of impressive learning that his half sister and aunt had been convinced would interest him in Lady Juno's companion, but he was willing to be patient. She spoke with a cultivated accent and her manner was reasonably elegant for one of her station, her attitude toward her mistress' complaints one of concern but not undue apprehension. Very proper, he thought. Perhaps that in and of itself indicated no mean intelligence.

The lady, however, from whom he felt a certain subtle air of antipathy emanating toward him was sitting on the other side of their hostess. She was engaged in conversation with Lady Fitzwarren, Cassandra Ramsay, and Lady Fredericks. All of them had met coincidentally on the steps in front of Lady Juno's town house.

Stealing a glance at her profile, St. John wondered if he had imagined Miss Pierce's aloofness when they had greeted each other on the street. Her demeanor was so pleasant now as she took part in the conversation going on between the others in the room. He had found himself divided from that conversation, having upon his entrance taken a seat next to Miss Gretehed when his hostess had indicated he ought. St.

John would have liked to test his intuition on the matter of Miss Pierce's reserve with him, but had not had the opportunity.

"—Sir St. John? Have you?"

St. John blinked. Woolgathering again. A week spent in solitude had done him no good in the end. This kind of behavior simply would not do.

"I beg your pardon, madam? A ringing in my ears, you know," he equivocated.

So much for making a good impression. He tried to smile, but the expression would not reach his eyes. Miss Gretehed did not seem to mind.

"Hippocrates, Sir St. John. Have you read his work on Nutriment?"

"I cannot say, ma'am."

" 'Nutriment is that which is nourishing; nutriment is that which is fit to nourish,' " she quoted, laying her hand on his arm very briefly. It was a well-shaped, long-fingered hand. "I have insisted to Lady Juno that it is not necessary to restrict oneself solely to broth and crackers when one suffers a lung complaint, for according to Hippocrates, 'The lungs draw a nourishment which is the opposite of that of the body, all other parts draw the same.' "

"Indeed? How interesting, Miss Gretehed."

"Indeed, Sir St. John, fascinating!" she said earnestly, turning on him gray eyes filled with enthusiasm. Intellectual passion. Now, this was something St. John thought he could safely appreciate.

"I have begged Lady Juno to take her nourishment more seriously, but she will not heed me. And I have urged her to move to a climate more suited to her constitutional needs," the companion explained, hands folded demurely in her lap. St. John watched as one of those hands reached to the piecrust table beside her and took from it a slim, red leather-bound volume. He could not make out the title printed in black embossed letters on the binding.

"I should like very much to read to you if I may, Sir St. John, from a recent translation of the Greek master's work on Airs, Waters, and Places," she said, looking without shyness at St. John as her fingers opened the little book. "Perhaps were you to advise me on how to convey this information to Lady Juno—she is uninterested in hearing me read from this to her, preferring her gazette—she would come to some understanding of what would be best for her."

"I am at your disposal, Miss Gretehed."

"Thank you, Sir St. John," she said, not without feeling. She bent her head to peer at the book. St. John noticed that the lady was squinting as she leafed through the pages in search of her place. Her hair was a nondescript brown color, but shining and smoothly combed into a modest knot at the back of her head. She moved her lips as she searched, seemingly speaking to herself to guide her fingers.

"Ah, here we are. I had passed it already," she explained, and moved the book rather close to her face and began to read. " 'A city that lies exposed to the hot winds—these are those between the winter rising of the sun and its winter setting—when subject to these and sheltered from the north winds, the waters here are plentiful and brackish, and must be near the surface, hot in summer and cold in winter.' " She raised her eyes. "I believe this is an excellent description of southeastern England, Sir St. John. But see what Hippocrates says of those who live here. 'The heads of the inhabitants are moist and full of phlegm, and their digestive organs are frequently deranged from the phlegm that runs down into them from the head. Most of them have a rather flabby physique, and they are poor eaters and drinkers—' "

St. John listened silently, only momentarily taking private umbrage at the suggestion of flabby physiques, given that he spent no little effort maintaining one that most definitely could not be described in such a way. Although he doubted the identification Miss Gretehed made of London, yet on the account of the "excessive fluxes" to which the women of such a region were often subject, he had less skepticism of the work's aptness. He glanced to his left as the lady continued to read.

Miss Pierce was sitting silently, eyes on her hands in her lap, apparently listening to a discussion between Lady Fredericks and Lady Fitzwarren. She must have felt his regard, for at the moment he was poised to turn his attention again to Miss Gretehed, Miss Pierce raised her head and her gaze met his squarely across the tea table. She saw him looking at her and a line creased her forehead. Then she looked away.

Excessive fluxes, indeed.

St. John could not imagine what he might have done to offend Miss Pierce, but offended it seemed she was. He had not seen her for over a week, several days, in fact, before he had taken to his house in seclusion after the night at Vaux-hall. Before that, they had been on the best of terms. She had been very pleasant at the Wentworths' musical evening, and he had—albeit at the cost of no trifling personal discomfort—maintained his very best behavior. Why she should now level such a cross look at him when the last time they had met she had seemed perfectly happy in his company, he could not guess. St. John had perused the betting books at his club that morning before making his way to his aunt's home. There were no new wagers, no further rumors linking her name with Fenton's. He knew not what cause she would have to regard him with such thinly veiled displeasure.

Repressing a sigh—he seemed these days always to be repressing something—he turned his attention once more on Miss Gretehed. He was just in time, for she had only just reached the end of a passage and was pausing to look at him.

"Ma'am, how is it that you became interested in the Greeks?" he asked with a successful attempt at imbuing his voice with sincere curiosity.

"I discovered at the lending library in Leeds a translation of a work of Aristotle on the physics of animal nature, Sir St. John," she explained. "When I came into Lady Juno's household and learned of her infirmity, I immediately began to seek out in the ancients a method for curing her. She was so very uncomfortable, you see. It is nothing, really. A hobby turned useful, I suppose."

She did not smile, but her expression mellowed, and St. John found himself thinking not for the first time how difficult the life of a hired servant must be, especially when one was born and bred to less onerous employment. He was favorably impressed that she had found ways to make her life bearable, and that she had gone to the ancients to seek advice. Not many young ladies of his acquaintance would have done such a thing in her place. But then, most young ladies of his acquaintance were not in her place. As their time was largely spent entertaining themselves, not others, and making themselves attractive to men, book learning did not normally come into the equation. St. John tried to imagine Felicia Strapley with a book in her hand, or Rosalind Hinde attempting to comfort an old, crotchety woman. He could not.

"I sympathize with your concern, ma'am, and commend you for it, as well as for your enthusiasm for the wisdom of the ancients."

"Thank you, sir. It is all I can do in this little life," Miss Gretehed replied with admirable humility, he thought. "Lady Juno's asthma grows worse when we are in London, but she has still a very strong constitution."

" 'Let it be as it pleases, provided there be no sigh from the soul.' Is that not right, Miss Gretehed?"

St. John and Miss Gretehed both turned their eyes on the speaker, who sat regarding them somewhat uncomfortably from across the table. St. John's mouth curved into a smile. There was a hesitation on Miss Pierce's lips, as if she felt some embarrassment for overhearing and interrupting their exchange. Nevertheless, it seemed to him that her hazel eyes were lit with sympathy and understanding.

"I do not entirely comprehend you, Miss Pierce."

St. John was surprised out of his contemplation of Alethea Pierce's extraordinarily expressive eyes by the cool tone of Miss Gretehed's voice. He noted the slight flush that rose to color the girl's cheeks, but she remained composed.

"My grandmother has been similarly unwell for several years, Miss Gretehed," she spoke in explanation. "I often go to visit her during the autumn and winter months, and believe she finds great comfort that, despite her illness, she has many years yet to enjoy life and what it brings to her. I have sometimes thought that those words of Seneca describe her attitude so aptly."

St. John contemplated Miss Pierce for a moment, then turned his eyes to Miss Gretehed. She seemed still uncertain what to say, but her demeanor had unbent somewhat.

"Yes, well, your grandmother sounds a fine lady, Miss Pierce."

The two regarded one another for a long moment, one with warm hazel eyes, the other from wary gray ones. Finally, St. John cleared his throat.

"We can all expect better health in the countryside, I doubt it not," he commented lightly. "Do you ladies take the waters in Bath or perhaps go to Brighton this summer?"

Miss Gretehed responded without hesitation.

"Lady Juno and I remove to Bath as soon as the weather merits it. The days are still cool enough in London that my mistress believes it too soon to depart here."

The moment had passed. Miss Gretehed's complexion was clear again. She was not a one to remain discommoded for long, he reflected with approval. He turned to Miss Pierce.

"And your family, Miss Pierce? Where do you go?" he asked.

"We are for Kent, sir." She turned then, without batting an eyelash, and began to speak to the women beside her as if she had never left their conversation. St. John felt, unaccountably, as if he had been slapped. Miss Gretehed seemed not to notice. He took a breath.

"What diversions does Lady Juno plan for you and she whilst habitating in Bath, Miss Gretehed?"

His voice was even. Of course it was even. Why ever should it not be?

Twelve

"Oh, do stop shouting, Tavy. I've taken the most devilish headache."

Alethea dragged herself up the staircase of their town house, temples pounding as she unlaced her bonnet and drew it from her head wearily. Reaching the upper story, she moved toward her room and entered it, dropping the bonnet on a chair and unfastening her pelisse before she deposited herself across the bed.

"Why, whatever is the matter with you, peagoose? Are you unwell?"

Alethea raised her head slightly to see her sister standing in the door to her room, and she lay back again.

"Not unwell precisely. Just tired, darling." She placed one arm across her eyes to shut out the dim sunlight coming through her partially drawn draperies. "Could you pull the curtains, Tavy? I would be much obliged."

Her sister moved over to the window and blocked out the remaining daylight with the drapery. The room was bathed in warm shadows, and Alethea felt the slightest bit better. She had slept very little the night before, blaming it on the quantity of champagne drunk at the ball she had attended until almost dawn. It had been the last Grande Fête of the Season. Before the week was out, London would be barren of Society, and everyone who was still about had attended the party hoping to eke out the very last pleasures the waning Season had to offer. It had been a sore crush, a stiflingly hot one, and Alethea had let herself drink too much and eat too little. She had been partnered the entire evening by numerous and enthusiastic gentlemen, had danced her feet and legs to exhaustion, and had had a miserable time.

The young viscount March had actually cornered her on the terrace early in the evening, ostensibly to tell her how much he *cared* for her; he had managed before the end of the brief interview to put his hands on her in several places where caring was not in the least an issue, she thought. She had defended herself rather nicely and trusted that the fellow now understood her feelings on the matter. Her knee still smarted, but she was proud that she had remembered the useful advice Horace Fredericks had once let slip to her when in a slightly foxed condition. Sir Pennworthy's lack of assistance on this occasion was not regretted in the least. Alethea could take care of herself. She was determined to do so for the rest of her life.

Only Belinda's presence had made the evening endurable, and the company of Cassandra and Timothy. But Alethea was glad the Season was finally over, and that she would be able to go home and never see another charming gentleman again as long as she lived. They flirted, they flattered, they made cows' eyes at her. None of them were sincere, none of them were subtle, none of them had a hint of knowledge of what real affection meant.

In such a humor, she knew she should not have gone out for her planned drive with Monsieur Le Maine and Belinda today, having felt wretched even after waking from her five hours of fitful sleep. But that gentleman had been so kind to her after her diatribe at Vauxhall, and so deferentially solicitous, she hated to be rude. Too, she imagined that Belinda would not approve her defection, Monsieur Le Maine's effusive company being rather wearing when one had to enjoy it alone. And so she had gone off with them to the Park despite the threatening ache in her head and the dark circles under her eyes.

She should have listened to her intuition. The day was exceedingly warm, even in the shade; and the paths of Hyde Park were still cluttered enough this late in the Season that progress had been slow, the breeze nonexistent. Alethea had been uncomfortable since leaving the house, but when they passed Sir Pennworthy driving Lady Juno and Miss Gretehed along the way, the day had gone from unpleasant to unbearable.

"You are not just tired," Alethea's sister came over and sat herself on the bed lightly. "You are blue-deviled," she said with decision. "What is it that is bothering you, Thea?"

"I assure you, darling, I am simply tired," Alethea responded. The partial truth was better than no truth at all, she supposed.

Octavia seemed to consider her statement, and

then, after a moment, she accepted it. She leaned back on the bed.

"I have just come from saying good-bye to Lilly and Esther," she commented, chewing on her nails as was sometimes her habit. Alethea lifted a hand off the coverlet to push her sister's fingers away from her mouth, but the effort was too much for her. She dropped her hand again and breathed deeply. "They are leaving on the morrow, and I admit I will miss them acutely. But Lady Fitzwarren has the most marvelous idea for a house party later this month, and assured us we would see each other then," the girl said cheerily.

If only all ills could be cured with a house party, Alethea thought. How good it must be to be a girl still. Then her brow furrowed. She winced at the movement.

"A house party?"

"Yes, isn't it famous?" Octavia sat up again. "Lady Fitzwarren says Stratford-upon-Avon is deathly dull in the summertime, and that she is determined to enliven it with a party at her estate. She intends to invite a great number of people, I understand. We, of course, are on the guest list." Alethea would have been amused at the hauteur in her sister's normally carefree voice, but she was in no mood to feel any such pleasant emotion.

"When is this party to be, Tavy?" Perhaps if it were late enough in the summer she could make the excuse that she wished to remain at home for the harvest. Or perhaps she could leave earlier than usual to visit her grandmother. Lady Fitzwarren's nephew was certain to be in attendance; Alethea did not know if she could stand the uncomfortable pleasure of that for the extended length of time a house party would last.

"Oh, probably in July," Octavia responded. "Lilly said it will serve as an occasion to announce St. John's betrothal, and so better sooner than later, or there will be no surprise in the matter at all."

Alethea suddenly found that she could not breathe.

"Betrothal?" she heard herself whisper, and then say more strongly as she struggled to gather her senses, "Is the baronet to be married, Tavy?"

"It appears so, although I do not believe he has asked Miss Gretehed quite yet." Octavia looked down at her prone sister. "Why, it ought not to come as a surprise to you, Thea. He has been hanging out for a wife for eons now, Lilly says. She says he could not see a dog in front of his face if it were to bite him on the nose, and he doesn't have any idea that there are a score of girls in Society that would welcome his suit, especially for his money, I suppose," she added lightly, appreciating a joke that Alethea could not quite fathom. "He believes only Miss Gretehed will have him, and will probably ask her soon enough. Perhaps even today. They were going driving in the Park today." Octavia pulled at a hangnail on her thumb and winced when it stung.

"Do you know why St. John has his own establishment here in Town, and not just a flat of apartments, like Horace Fredericks or Toby Wisterly?" the girl asked, obviously knowing the answer and wishing to impart it. Alethea, barely aware of the words her lips chose to form, responded, "No, dear. Because he is not a sad rattle like they are?"

Octavia made a crack of laughter. Alethea did not know why.

"No, silly! Lilly says it is because he has wanted a wife for heaven knows how long, and bought a house for the day when he should get one. He has asked several ladies to marry him already, it seems, but cannot seem to find one who will say yes." She shook her red braids in sympathetic amusement. "Poor fellow. Sir St. John's top-of-the-trees, it's true, and Lilly and Esther adore him, but *he* is something of a rattle, don't you think? No wonder he is going to settle for a lady's companion."

Alethea looked up at her sister for a long moment and then, slowly, she sat up on the bed. She put her hand on Octavia's arm, and the girl glanced down at it before she looked again with surprise at her older sister.

"Tavy, Miss Gretehed is a lady, as much as we are ladies," Alethea said evenly. "If Sir St. John, who is a respectable gentleman, should deem her a suitable choice for a wife, then we should trust that he has insight into her character that perhaps we lack. I should not like to hear you refer so rudely again to a lady who has only been a bit unlucky in life. Do you perfectly understand me?"

Alethea watched her sister nod slowly, chastened, and she dropped her hand.

"Good," she said. "Now, darling, would you mind very much closing the door after you leave? I should like to rest before dinner."

Alone in her room, the brightness of the hot, early summer day shut out by the heavy curtains, Alethea stared up at the lace-bedecked canopy above her.

He was to be married. Something must have told her that; she must have known it somehow in her heart even before Octavia said the words. She had never felt so wretched before as she had when she had seen him this afternoon, all merely because he accompanied an old lady and her companion for a drive in the Park. Now she knew why.

Alethea spared a momentary thought for the exquisite she had seen him with at Vauxhall those weeks ago, wondering what had happened to her. He had asked other women to wed, Lilly had disclosed to Octavia. Was that beautiful widow one of them? It seemed unlikely, but who could know? He had asked Alethea herself on no more than a minute's acquaintance; anything was possible, she supposed. Why, then, had he waited almost two weeks to ask Miss Gretehed? For that was how long he had known her already, for certain. Alethea remembered their introduction, the calculating look in Lady Juno's eyes as she made them acquainted with each other in her drawing room, the way the sick old woman had insisted he sit by her companion to assist in pouring out the tea.

Alethea had been in a poor humor that afternoon as soon as she had set eyes on Sir Pennworthy in the street in front of Lady Juno's house. She had not got over seeing him in the pleasure gardens with the beautiful widow, nor had she liked not meeting him at all for so many days after that. Octavia had not happened to let fall any information as to his whereabouts that week, and Alethea had found herself imagining that he had eloped with the widow.

Of course, now that she thought of it, her reaction had been foolish. She had told herself at the time that she was just disgusted with him, her disgust for all men simply spilling over onto him now that she had good cause for it. But she had misjudged her own motivations. After seeing him at Vauxhall and then missing his company for a week, she had been angry, true, but for an entirely different reason. In fact, she had believed that his absence in her life was due to the fact that he was so caught up with that other, mature, beautiful woman that he had entirely forgotten about *her*. No matter that he had proposed to Alethea once, too, in a time that now seemed long, long ago.

The knowledge that she had not been the only one was, surprisingly, quite painful. She realized now that she had been holding the secret of his offer to herself as something special that connected them. Now, knowing that she was not unique to him in this perverse way, that gossamer connection was cut in two. Instead, she was just what any of the other girls were who sighed when he smiled and wished he would do it more often in their direction. She was just what the men who gave her their unwanted attentions thought her to be. She was a silly fool.

" 'So we endured two inconveniences at the same time, and they were diametrically different:

we struggled both with mud and with dust on the same road and on the same day.' "

"Whatever can you mean, Sir St. John?"

He grew fonder of her each day. It had been wise to wait and come to know her, to be patient. She was not typically high-spirited nor easily distractible like younger ladies. She was nearer to his own age than the schoolroom, and he appreciated the maturity she displayed on all occasions. If she rarely questioned him thus, looking upon him as if he had just sprung horns and a tail, how could he complain that she did so at all?

They were walking slowly through the Park. The day was still young, and as it had rained heavily overnight the paths sparkled here and there with puddles that only now, as the sun climbed higher into the sky, were beginning to disappear.

"I beg your pardon, Miss Gretehed. As you had just told me of the difficulties with weather you and Lady Juno experienced last year on your way to Bath, I thought to make a reference to Seneca, his letter On the Trials of Travel." He smiled slightly at her, noting as usual that she was not blushing. She never blushed. "I thought perhaps you would recognize it. I recall you quoted from Seneca's Epistles just the other day, his letter On Worldliness and Retirement."

Miss Gretehed's expression did not change, but he thought her lips tightened a bit before she replied.

"Yes, well, I must have forgotten that other letter. Sometimes I read very late at night, when I am rather tired, you see."

St. John saw a great deal more than his companion knew. Miss Gretehed's knowledge of the classical authors she so often professed a devotion for was not what she represented it to be. She tended to repeat the same quotations over and over again—which was not to be dismissed, of course; they had lasted thousands of years, and repetition did them no harm. He had, however, just that morning uncovered a little book in the parlor of Lady Juno's house that proved upon closer inspection not to be Hippocrates, but was instead entitled *Forty Steps to Improving a Gentleman's Conversation*. In it, St. John had been interested to see, were English translations of quotations, taken entirely out of context, of every one of the authors Miss Gretehed had herself quoted over the past two and a half weeks. He had not been able to read more before Lady Juno appeared to greet him, but he had not needed to.

He did not disrespect Miss Gretehed for her limited knowledge. She was a woman and few women were fortunate enough to receive training in ancient literature as men of his class so often did. Not often enough, of course, or the publishers of *Forty Steps* had no business. No, her interest commended her to him, instead. But he could not like her dishonesty. Pretense of any sort did not sit well with St. John.

He had not meant to bring up his discovery, in any way, and especially not in such a churlishly tricky manner. She was a fine individual. Intelligent, if not schooled. She had good conversation—even disregarding the quotations with which she peppered it—and a devotion to Lady

Juno that was quite impressive. She would consider the bonds of marriage a responsibility not to be taken lightly. He could not ask for more, nor could he condemn her for wanting to be better than what she was. Did not most people? He himself was a prime example. He had no right to tease her.

In fact, the quotation had come into his head the night before on his way home from dinner at his club. When slogging through the chilling rain, he had recalled how just that afternoon the same London street had been stifling with heavy heat. He had wanted to share his humor in the situation. But not with Miss Gretehed. He had wanted to tell Miss Alethea Pierce, whose knowledge of Seneca he somehow could not imagine came from a book on conversational skills.

More the fool, he. Someone, it seemed, had won the wager concerning that lady and the lascivious Mr. Fenton. Brooks's betting book did not make it clear which side had taken the stake, but understanding Miss Pierce's character one would have to be a veritable fool not to know she had accepted a proposal of marriage. In the end, the lout Fenton had won the true prize.

"If the roads should be clear, then you will leave for Bath on Thursday, ma'am?" he asked, turning the conversation back to the weather and her traveling plans.

"It is Lady Juno's wish that we do so," his companion replied. She turned her face to him. "I have so enjoyed these last weeks, Sir St. John. I thank you for your escort and company. They have been very refreshing to me."

St. John felt his throat constrict. He slowed his

pace and raised his hand to take Miss Gretehed's
and tuck it under his arm.

"Miss Gretehed, I should like to ask you something," he said evenly. "I have also enjoyed our
brief acquaintance. It would be my greatest pleasure to continue it in a more intimate fashion."

For a lady of understanding and maturity, she
certainly reacted with fervent alacrity when
moved. St. John stood stunned by his smarting
face as he attempted to understand why he had
been slapped—and rather hard, at that—by the
woman standing now several feet away from him
who had moments ago expressed her great pleasure in his company.

"Sir," Miss Gretehed said with a slightly trembling voice. "I may be a servant, but I have not
fallen so desperately beneath my station as to welcome a slip on the shoulder. You insult me
gravely! I should not have expected you, a gentleman of such delicacy and refinement, to treat
me so shabbily. But I discover now I must have
been sorely misguided in judging your character." There was a bit of color in her face, spots
of red high on each smooth cheek.

St. John swallowed.

"I believe, madam, that perhaps you have mis-
understood me." His voice was neutral. "I was
attempting to ask you, actually, to be my wife."

It was gratifying and not a little amusing, he
was chagrined to admit, the transformation that
overtook the lady's expression in the course of
the next minute. When her eyes were finally
clear of the development of her thoughts, they
focused once again on him. St. John's brows rose
slightly.

"Is this an agreeable idea to you, madam?"

The smile she gave him, a combination of embarrassment and gratification, was affecting. St. John felt almost human.

It struck him as a rather odd idea that he had perhaps not been so before.

"Sir, it is quite agreeable," Miss Gretehed responded, looking very fetching in her gratification. "I am honored. I apologize for abusing you so. I am ashamed to have accused you of such a thing."

He was perversely content to see that she was not too overset by her mistake, nor by his proposal. She was clearly very pleased, but he had guessed before she was not one to fly into transports about anything, even such an offer. This suited St. John. He had had quite enough of emotion. Now he wanted only the companionship that he had craved his entire life. The companionship of a kind and intelligent human being.

"Do not think of it, ma'am," he replied, feeling a contentment steal into him that had nothing of passion or excitement in it, but much of relief. "I am glad I was able to make myself more clear before I received a blackened eye."

Miss Gretehed looked quizzingly at him and he silenced the sigh that tried to escape. He held out his arm and she took it, and they continued on the path in companionable silence.

"Should you like me to make our engagement known to Lady Juno?" he asked after a few moments, and was rewarded with a gasp from the woman at his side.

"My lady! Oh, sir!"

St. John turned to his betrothed repressing yet another sigh. "Is something amiss, Miss Gretehed?"

She turned suddenly anxious gray eyes on him.

"Sir, I do not know what I shall do," she said rather unsteadily for one of her usual calm. "Lady Juno is quite unable to get along on her own, and I do not know how I can leave her alone at this difficult time."

"Difficult time?"

Miss Gretehed lifted her hand to her mouth, pressing her fist against her lips in worried thought before answering.

"She suffers a new ailment, Sir St. John, one which we have not seen before last week." She looked at him. "I am certain I can be of help in this. The doctors have taught me how best to care for her, how to administer her medicine, what foods she is able to eat, how she is meant to take the air once every day but not for too long. Her recovery is certain, but only if she follows a very careful regimen." Her tone was sober. "But she will not do these things independently, sir. She is headstrong and stubborn—I take a distant relative's prerogative in admitting so without overstepping my bounds—and will not behave as she ought."

St. John covered her hand with his own again.

"It is commendable to be so concerned. She has been a friend to you and you have a caring and conscientious heart," he said. "Surely, however, she can be fitted with another companion who will take on the responsibilities which have weighed heavily on your shoulders. Perhaps you

can assist her in this, make both of them comfortable before you move away."

"Move away?" They had stopped walking
again, but he retained her hand against his arm.
He watched her shake her head slightly. "Sir St.
John, this is very troublesome to think of. Your
offer is welcome to me, but I shall need some
time to become accustomed to this engagement
and the change my life will endure."

He smiled with compassion into her anxious
eyes and patted her hand gently.

"Of course, madam. As you wish."

Thirteen

There were six women in the room. One sat fretting not altogether silently in a cushioned chair by the cold hearth. Another, much younger, attempted to calm the nerves of the first with lavender water and burnt rosemary, but was shooed impatiently away. Two others stood by the window to the street, speaking in hushed voices. Another sat on the edge of her seat, her hand resting on the shoulder of the last woman, whose own hands covered a face streaked with tears.

"Oh, how I should wish to be alone now, Lindy," Alethea said in a weak whisper to her best friend, drawing her palms away from her dampened cheeks and eyes.

"I know it, darling," whispered Miss Wisterly with compassion. "But we must wait until your father returns. You do not want to miss the news he has to tell us." She pressed a dry kerchief into her friend's palm.

Alethea focused eyes tired from weeping on her friend, and her shoulders slumped yet more.

"I *do* want to miss it, Lindy. I want to miss everything, including what has already happened," she said, controlling the sob she felt rising again in her chest by biting down on her lower lip. "I cannot fathom what ill fortune and wretched discernment I have had to bring me— us!—to this conclusion. I am entirely to blame for it, and that is what is so dreadful. For my dear father will have to pay for my foolishness." Her voice trembled, but she did not wish to continue to burden even her best friend with her miseries and self-pity. So she withheld the tears that yet threatened to fall even now after hours of weeping.

"You must stop saying so, Alethea," Belinda insisted quietly. "The man is a villain, and you could not know he would do such a thing, no matter what good a judge of character you are. And you are one, I know. You have chosen me as a friend, have you not?"

Alethea looked up at the other girl's grinning face and tried to smile. Her lips trembled and she could not manage it.

"Belinda, you are a saint. I shall miss you when I go into exile."

Miss Wisterly sat back in her chair, crossing her arms.

"Now you are playing at being Mrs. Siddons. I shall not comfort you any longer."

Alethea, trying to steady her features, blew her nose on the now sopping handkerchief.

"I am, as it is the only way I can stand this," she said softly, not daring to gaze at the compassion she knew shone in the other girl's eyes.

"He has returned," they heard from across the room, and Cassandra Ramsay and her mother stepped away from the window to move toward where Alethea and Belinda were by the door.

They sat in two of the only seats unshrouded by Holland covers. The family had been packed and nearly ready to depart the city when the news had arrived with Lady Fredericks, who had heard it from her modiste that morning.

From where she sat in the middle of her parlor, Mrs. Pierce emitted a groaning cry, and her younger daughter hastened with a vial of smelling salts to her side. Alethea did not see the look that passed between Miss Wisterly and the Fredericks women, for her eyes were glued to the door through which her father would walk.

A moment later the door to the parlor opened and Mr. Thaddeus Pierce entered, looking rather more serious than anyone present had ever before seen him. He was usually quite a jovial fellow, who, when he was not sleeping, was laughing at one thing or another. The six women in the room turned to face him as the butler closed the door behind him. Mr. Pierce came into the middle of the room and took his eldest daughter's hand.

"Thea, my darling daughter. I am sorry." His voice was steady, but just barely.

She looked up at him, holding onto his hand tightly.

"Papa, what has happened?"

He held her hand for a moment more and then, looking down at her with a painful smile, he patted it once and released it. He stepped over to the fireplace and spoke at large to the room.

"Fenton will meet me the morning after tomorrow at dawn, as is fitting."

"Oh, Papa!"

"Thaddeus, my husband!"

Alethea said nothing as she watched her father turn to her mother and bend to comfort her. Octavia put her arm around his back and buried her face in the shoulder of his coat.

"Bertram Fenton is reputed to be a poor shot and a mediocre swordsman. Which weapon has he chosen, Mr. Pierce?" Lady Fredericks was all business. Alethea thanked God that someone in the room was able to hold together. Belinda was right. It was best to have their friends around them at this time.

Alethea's father drew away from his wife and breathed deeply.

"Pistols, I am glad to say, Lady Fredericks," he replied less than enthusiastically. "I was concerned that as a younger man he would have the advantage over me with foils, and I am not ashamed to admit I am rather relieved he chose otherwise."

Alethea could not believe what she was hearing. She stood shakily and bit her lips before speaking as evenly as she could.

"Papa, you cannot do this," she said. "I would forbid it if I could, but instead I beg you. Please do not meet Mr. Fenton. I am willing to live with what he has said of me. I refuse to let you put yourself in this danger to save something as ridiculous as my reputation."

"Alethea!"

"Mother," she turned on her parent, "would you rather have Papa dead or me ruined? You have two choices only. I would recommend you not be missish about it." Her voice was hard.

"That will be quite enough, Alethea," she

heard her father say not ungently as he moved over to his wife again. "The challenge has been issued. For my honor, it cannot be rescinded now."

"What?" Alethea said, "For some grand principle you would not cancel this thing that is abominable to all of us? Papa, what can you mean?"

"Alethea, I have done what I have done. I expect you to abide by my wishes."

Alethea stared into her father's face for a moment, horrified. But in her heart she knew that, given the insult his daughter had received in public, he could not do otherwise and still maintain his honor. She walked over to him, took his hands in hers, and raised them to her cheek.

"I am so sorry, Papa. If I could have foreseen what he would do, I would have done everything in my power to stop him."

Mr. Pierce freed one hand and caressed his daughter's bent head with gentle fingers. He bent forward and kissed her on her brow, which was furrowed in deep distress.

"I know, my dear," he said tenderly. "Now, however, we shall just have to see it through to its end."

Timothy Ramsay had seen this expression on the face of one of his friends before. It was a look at once of loathing and determination. But when he had seen it the first time, it had included a weary sort of resignation. The man wearing the expression then had been responding to an insult to the girl he loved only because it was, in the end, the only thing he could honorably do.

St. John Pennworthy's expression did not share that resignation. Instead, Lord Bramfield read outrage and white-hot anger in every line of the blond man's visage.

"Why Fenton should wish to ruin such a gracious girl, I cannot fathom," Timothy said finally, almost afraid to wait for his friend to speak. He had been, indeed, quite taken aback at first by the baronet's violent reaction to the news. "It is entirely to his discredit that he has spread this rumor, for rumor Cassandra assures me it truly is." He regarded the other man thoughtfully for a moment, and then added, "Women tell each other the truth of these things, you know."

St. John did not know anything at that moment. He only felt. And the fury inside of him was beyond anything he had ever experienced before.

"When is Fenton to meet her father?"

The viscount felt an entirely unfamiliar frisson of nerves run up his forearms at the grinding menace in his friend's normally prosaic voice. He almost looked around the room to see if someone else had spoken.

"Day after tomorrow—at dawn, of course." He watched as St. John finally moved from the statue-still position he had been standing in, stepped over to his desk, and opened a drawer. He pulled out a leather purse and an oil-wrapped object that looked suspiciously to Timothy like a pistol. Lord Bramfield's gaze shifted warily from the desktop, where these things had been deposited, to Sir Pennworthy's face.

"You are not responsible for the girl, St. John," he said slowly, distinctly enunciating each word. "You have no business in this mess."

St. John raised his midnight-dark eyes to his old friend, and Timothy had the distinct feeling that he was not what the man was seeing in that moment.

"The hell I don't."

It was simple enough to make the arrangements to have Bertram Fenton meet him the following night at the Docks in a warehouse with which St. John was very familiar. Money was a neat enticement for everything, he had learned years ago, especially to a man who used a great deal of it yet had little. It was more difficult, at such short notice, to gather the information needed to fulfill his plans for the lying profligate. St. John employed both his valet and the footman who acted as butler in his bachelor's home in addition to his tiger to seek out and acquire the necessary material. St. John himself had had to visit no fewer than a dozen taverns on the East Side and spend a purse full of guineas before he came away with the knowledge and proof he required to fix the man for good.

It had not been easy, but it had not been terribly difficult, either. Fenton was a rough customer, it seemed, when it came to both liquor and wenches. He was not especially liked in the establishments in which he often took his pleasure; one young woman he had recently visited, and who still had bruises on the side of her face and neck to prove it, went so far as to offer to go to the law for St. John. St. John, of course, refused her help—it would have meant the girl's certain arrest—but the conviction had grown in him that he was doing right. This was despite the fact that it was none of his personal business, as his friend Bramfield and his own conscience told him countless times. But what St. John in the end found out about Fenton had quickly done away with any of those concerns.

Dark fell early that night, aided in its arrival by thick gray thunderclouds gathering in the west and then spreading above the city, obscuring the stars that still valiantly attempted to peek through the smog. St. John stood along one empty wall of his warehouse, counting slowly the droplets of water he heard fall from a leak in the ceiling onto the scuffed wood at his feet. He would have to have that leak fixed before the next shipment arrived. Silk did not take kindly to damp.

He heard his guest before he saw him emerge from the doorway closest to the street. He watched a rat the size of a lady's lapdog precede Fenton out of the passageway at a gallop. St. John pushed himself away from the wall where he had been leaning, and walked out into the middle of the vast empty space to meet the man. Two lanterns burned at either side of the building, casting wavering yellow light on the space and throwing St. John's face into shadow where he stood. Naturally, the effect had been carefully planned.

It was successful. Bertram Fenton looked about him, as if suspicious of some kind of trap. St. John smiled, knowing now at the end of the busy day that the man had reason to be so paranoiac.

"I am so glad you could come," St. John said pleasantly, as if he greeted the man at the door of his house and not here in the dark stench of the London shipyard. He drew out a pipe from his waistcoat pocket, tamped down the tobacco—his own, naturally, although he rarely smoked the stuff—and raised the pipe to his mouth. Effect was everything.

"What is it you have to offer me, Pennworthy?" the other man said, none too congenially. St. John sighed silently. How *had* she come to see anything admirable in this mannerless clod?

"Offer, Mr. Fenton? Why, what made you think I had something to offer you?" He struck a match and lit the pipe, gathering sufficient smoke in the next few silent moments to tinge the dimly lit space with fantastical shapes. St. John had never himself much liked to smoke, but he had always found those smoke shapes marvelous. His great-grandfather had used to make them for him when he was a boy.

"Do not play dolt with me, man. Your message said you had a proposal you wished to make, is that not the case?" Fenton was feeling more confident now, had crossed his arms before him and planted his booted feet in an imposing stance. His legs were thick with muscle. But he did not frighten St. John. The baronet had once already taken good measure of Bertram Fenton's pugilistic talents. The man was all ire and no finesse. St. John sucked on his pipe and blew out a cloud of smoke. He tapped his fingers on the bowl.

"Come to think on it, Fenton," he drawled, "I do have a proposal to make you." He inhaled again, and then puffed out. "Clever of you to drop in tonight just when I wanted to ask it of you."

Fenton was not easily perturbed.

"And . . . ?" he asked with practiced patience. A man did not achieve the success at fraud and raking that this man had without knowing how to bide his time. But his voice held a tinge of condescension, as if he were speaking to a child, or a simpleton. St. John found he did not like that very much. He decided to come to the point more quickly than he had intended.

"I am an honest businessman, Fenton," he said, reaching into his waistcoat pocket and drawing forth a small stack of papers. "I manufacture and grow and buy and sell, and I make a hefty profit at it all—but honestly." His voice was conversational. "Bought myself a title recently with some of those profits, you may have heard."

St. John heard the other man snort, and he looked up now with distaste from the papers he was perusing. Presently he looked down again and continued.

"With that title, I have found, come more responsibilities than I already had before. One of these new responsibilities is seeing that the people who live in my district not suffer from the likes of such men as you, who make their money according to principles less honorable than those to which I hold myself accountable."

St. John stepped forward into the light and looked straight at the other man.

"I understand you spent some time near Exeter two summers ago, is that not correct, Mr. Fenton?"

"What is it you want, Pennworthy? I will not

stay here and listen to this nonsense, if that is what you intend." Fenton was growing angry. His arms were no longer crossed. They hung at his sides, fists clenched.

"Bear with me, please, just for a moment," St. John said, moving through the papers in his hand deliberately until he reached the one he sought. "Ah, yes, Fenton. You *were* indeed in Exmouth, not far from some property I have there, the summer those two girls were found murdered by the mill house, is that not so?"

"You—"

"You were visiting—correct me if I mistake it— Lady Droughton in the next district over, I believe. Her husband was elsewhere, at his dying mother's bedside, and you went to comfort the baroness in her time of loneliness and grief, if I understand correctly."

"Pennworthy, you are making trouble where you do not want it." Fenton's voice was menacing.

"Oh, forgive me, sir," St. John said lightly. "I had thought *you* were the one who made the trouble on that occasion." He let fall the hand that held the papers and stared into the eyes of the other man, his mouth suddenly a thin, white line. "Aside from your numerous fraudulent financial schemes, Fenton, and several petty crimes you have committed here in London, in Exmouth you erred beyond the acceptable. For this, I find myself unusually irritated with you, and wish to offer an unequaled solution to your having murdered those girls."

"You will never make it stick, Pennworthy. You are out of your league. You ought to keep your head in the Shop and stop nosing into business that don't concern you, you simple-minded Cit."

"Tut-tut, Fenton," St. John said between clenched teeth, "your manners are slipping." He gestured into the darkness and two men, who by their burly build and rough appearance proclaimed themselves to be regulars of the Docks, stepped out into the light on either side of Fenton. Another man followed them into the pool of yellow light. He wore a red vest and held a pistol, which was trained on the dark-haired gentleman.

"What are you going to do, Pennworthy? Bring me up before the Bench? You will never be able to prove a thing, and my father will drag your name through the mud when it is all through." Fenton glanced to either side of himself, assessing whether he could escape or not. "You shall have to hide in India, or wherever other barbarous place you spent your dubious youth, and you will never be able to see your precious Miss Pierce again. Don't think I don't know that this is why you are threatening me like this." He looked tauntingly at St. John now, a sneer on what may have been considered by some his handsome face.

"She was a choice bit when she finally came panting to me, Pennworthy. Every bit the luscious little trollop, from her—"

St. John had not intended to hit the man. He had hoped to pass this evening without even raising his voice. But he could not allow the knave to continue. Not in the hearing of his two employees and a Bow Street Runner. A gentleman had his limits, after all.

"Now, now, laddie, ya dinna hav'ta be doin' that, now did ya?"

Henry O'Flannery, the red-vested gentleman, gazed down at the blustering nobleman on his back on the floor, and stretched out a hand to help him up.

"Please forgive me, O'Flannery. I was carried away." St. John bowed slightly and straightened his coat.

Bertram Fenton was on his feet again, only restrained from lunging at St. John by the presence of the two men lounging casually against the wall several yards off, and the Runner's gun still pointed at dead aim on his chest. He affected a pose of nonchalance instead.

"I shall be out of Newgate the moment you put me there, Pennworthy. You needn't even attempt it," he said very calmly. If he did not despise the man so, St. John thought he might be impressed.

"You are a fool, Fenton," he said flatly, dropping the pretense of conviviality. "Only a fool—albeit a desperate one—would have come here tonight."

Fenton looked at St. John as if he had gotten the whole thing backward.

"You are as daft as they say, Pennworthy. You cannot touch me."

The two men regarded each other for a long moment, neither blinking for what seemed to be hours.

"Seems t'me, laddie, like'n he alreddy 'as teched ya," came the Runner's voice from beside them, accompanied by a chuckle. St. John felt his mouth curl up at the edge, involuntarily.

" 'N I'm here te tell ya, he's not only got the proof 'n witnesses te look ya away, but te 'ang ya, me boy, sure'n as my pappy's name weren't Ooley O'Flannery."

Fenton looked to the little man with disdain, but the Irishman continued before he could speak.

"But I've a right mind not te let ya 'ave that 'angin' chance, laddie," he said, hooking the thumb of his free hand underneath the red wool of his waistcoat. "Ye sees, the guvnor here's got anither idea fer ya, and I likes it bitter n' bitter the more I sees of ya."

Fenton turned his wary gaze on St. John, and the blond man shrugged.

"I've had enough of your blood on my hands already, Fenton," he said, glancing at the man's swelling nose and then at his own knuckles. "The idea O'Flannery speaks of—the offer I am making to you tonight—has to do with you taking a very long journey, departing shortly, in fact. A journey from which I tend to believe you will never return."

Bertram Fenton began to move slowly backward, toward the entrance from which he had come. One of St. John's men stepped quickly to the opening to block his way.

"What are you talking about, Pennworthy? Are you mad? You are, you are mad and have always been." Fenton still moved backward, unaware of the man several feet behind him.

"You are going to Australia, Fenton. On one of my best ships," St. John said. "I hope you will not mind if you are not given the best room. It's mine, you see, or my captain's when I am not on board, and I would rather not have it disturbed. You do understand? In any case, it's a far better passage than you'd have on a galley." He shrugged and stepped forward, following the retreating figure.

" 'N a sight bitter accommodations than on the hulks, me laddie," added O'Flannery sagely, but St. John's gaze did not move from Fenton's.

"I am not going anywhere on any damned ship of yours, you crazy fool," spluttered the dark-haired man. "You cannot send me anywhere I—" He stepped into the dockworker behind him, and the man's muscle-bound arms clamped around his neck and chest. Fenton fought back for a moment, and then was suddenly still, his breath rasping as he glared viciously at St. John.

"You will not be back, if that is what you are thinking," St. John said with a slight shake of his head. "You are never, ever coming back. I suggest you get used to the idea very quickly, or it will be that much the worse for you. After all," he added, "a man like you could make quite a name for himself among louts and thieves." He gestured with his hand and the Runner stepped forward and clouted the captive on the back of the head with the butt of his revolver. Fenton's eyes flickered shut and he went limp in the dockworker's arms.

St. John and O'Flannery followed Clem and Joshua out onto the dock with their unconscious prisoner, bound with ropes. The baronet and Bow Street Runner saw to the safe and secure stowage of the unconscious nobleman in a tiny cabin at the bow of the ship. After a last few words with his captain, St. John accompanied the Runner through his warehouse once again and out onto the street where his carriage waited.

"The ship will sail shortly. My men are accustomed to such necessities, and the moon is full." St. John looked up into the night sky, surprising himself at the sight of the clear silver light shining on the dockyard and buildings around them. The thunderclouds of earlier had entirely disappeared, as if they had never been. He handed the Runner the papers from his waistcoat pocket.

"It's a root good thin' ya'v done, laddie, 'n that's fer shoore," the Runner said thoughtfully. "Eye'd bin' searchin' the country fer the man who killed them girls. Woulda' foond 'im sooner n' later, and strung 'im up. Ye get a bone a' mercy in there wi' yar heart, me boy, fer sendin' 'im off leke thet te live."

St. John stared into the sky at the moon, hovering over the water's edge like a giant beacon.

"I've been where he's going, Mr. O'Flannery, and I can assure you, it is not life at all to which I'm sending him."

Fourteen

"He did not *show*?"

"He did *not* show. Is it not marvelous? Mr. Pierce waited for three quarters of an hour before he sent the surgeon and his second home and returned home himself. What a coward that terrible man has turned out to be! He knew he wronged Alethea, and he was not honorable enough to stand by his own perfidy."

Miss Belinda Wisterly twirled her parasol in her hand gaily, smiling broadly. Cassandra Ramsay and her mother's old butler exchanged concerned looks, and the flaxen-haired viscountess reached out and took her friend's parasol from her hand and gave it to the man. She took Belinda's arm.

"Come into the parlor, Belinda. Lady Fitzwarren has just arrived and will be anxious to hear your story as well." She gave the butler a brief smile and led Miss Wisterly up the stairs to where her mother and the countess were sitting together.

"Miss Wisterly, tell us what you have heard," Lady Fredericks said as soon as the two young women entered the room. Belinda and Cassan-

dra walked over to the sofa and seated themselves across from the elder women.

"Alethea is justified! Mr. Fenton forfeited. He
did not appear at the appointed hour, and after
almost an hour had passed Mr. Pierce and Sir
Foster called forfeit, and they left," she explained as her friend poured her a cup of steaming tea and put it on the table before her.
Belinda took no note of it; her excitement at the
exoneration of her dearest friend was evident.

"Bertram Fenton did not show, you say?" Lady
Fitzwarren's black eyes were narrowed. "That
does not sound like the man."

Lady Fredericks nodded. With a pensive expression, she leaned forward to take up her tea,
and lifted it to her lips to sip. "No, it does not,
does it, Mellicent? For all he is despicable, Fenton is the son of a nobleman and would not
lightly fail to discharge this score of honor," she
said thoughtfully. She raised her eyes to Belinda.
"Has he been heard of today? Does anyone know
of his whereabouts?"

"He has not been seen since last evening," Belinda responded readily. "Mr. Pierce made in-
quiries at Mr. Fenton's club, in case there had
been some mistake of the morning's meeting
place. Sir Foster found Mr. Fenton's second hid-
ing there, himself ignorant as to where his friend
had gone, but too afraid to admit to it for fear
he should have to meet Alethea's father instead."
She looked around at the other women. "Is it
not fantastic, that Fenton would have disappeared from Town without even alerting his second to his plans?"

"Fantastic, indeed," Lady Fredericks said, her tone shrewd. "Where was he last seen?"

"Some gentlemen at the club said that a message for him had arrived there in the afternoon brought by a street boy. Mr. Pierce found out that no one seemed to know from whom the message came, but that Mr. Fenton seemed perfectly content with it. He left the club without telling any of his friends where he was going." Belinda looked from one matron to the other, brow furrowed. "Could something be amiss? Is Alethea's reputation not saved by Fenton's forfeiture and flight from Town?"

"It is odd, unquestionably so," Lady Fredericks responded, seeming to have come to some conclusion in her thoughts. "However, that the man forfeited can only reflect well on Alethea's situation. Before the Season begins next year this will all be long forgotten, a nine days' wonder, I doubt it not."

The two young ladies in the room released the breaths they had been holding anxiously, and exchanged relieved looks. Mellicent Fitzwarren sipped her tea pensively, and when Lady Bramfield and Miss Wisterly looked at her for confirmation of Lady Fredericks's opinion, she nodded. But when Cassandra followed Belinda into the hall to see her out after the visit, Lady Fitzwarren turned to her friend, black eyes pinpoints under her pink-and-red striped turban.

"Hecuba?" she said, and bit into a plum tart. She chewed for a moment while Lady Fredericks poured more tea. "Do you think the man forfeited, or—how shall I say it?—*was* forfeited?"

"By the way, Mellicent," Lady Fredericks responded, as if she had not heard her friend, "I have been meaning to tell you that I passed your nephew on the street yesterday. He did not see me, as he seemed particularly preoccupied with something."

She glanced at Lady Fitzwarren, who was looking at her over the rim of her teacup.

"It was the oddest thing, really. Such a nice boy, St. John, when he has his head out of the clouds. But it overset me somewhat to see him like that. You know, Mellicent, I could have sworn yesterday that he was being chased by the devil himself."

St. John walked slowly across the green of Berkeley Square, cutting north for a block before turning the corner to Lady Juno's street. He had been walking for some time now in circles around London. The day was fine, if a bit on the warm side to be entirely comfortable. The sun was glowing hazily between white, fluffy clouds; the trees and flowers were blossoming on every street and in every green along the way.

He was rather weary, if truth be told. He was accustomed to walking, but not so much as he had today. When he last examined his watch the time had been four o'clock, more than three hours since he had left the Pierces' house on Abbey Street.

St. John halted at the end of a block, in sight of Lady Juno's residence.

Gracious, but the time flew by, did it not? He had not been thinking for all of that time, of course. Mostly just walking. His boots were feeling a bit snug, a bit warm, too. His hands were cold, though. Had been cold all day long. He hoped Miss Pierce had not noticed that when he had taken hers to shake, wishing her a happy summer and good-bye.

He had gone over to the Pierces' house to say farewell, since they were leaving Town this very afternoon. Alethea Pierce had remained in the hall a moment longer than her sister and mother, for what reason he knew not, and had asked him if they would see him at his aunt's party the next month. St. John had said no, he had business that would make his attendance there impossible.

Lying always turned his hands to ice. He was a terrible liar. Withholding a truth was quite disagreeable in its own way, but outright lying was awful.

He could not promise to be at Lady Fitzwarren's party, for it was very possible that Miss Gretehed would wish to remain with Lady Juno until a replacement for her could be arranged. If that were to be the case, St. John would remain in Town, or remove to Bath when the two women did. It was only proper that he should do so. Miss Gretehed had suggested as much, as well. But he had not been able to tell Miss Pierce that.

Her hazel eyes had regarded him solemnly but her lips had smiled when she had bid him adieu. Remarkable how she was able to make such an expression. He always felt entirely transparent in his emotions, but she managed to be quite ambiguous with hers. Not inconsistent or deceptive. Simply ambiguous.

She was an unusual young woman, Miss

Alethea Pierce. He had enjoyed their conversations very much. And he had other things he yet wanted to discuss with her. Seneca, gardens, beekeeping . . . and, for instance, he would have liked to quiz her about her most recent thoughts on Mr. Bertram Fenton.

St. John laughed derisively at himself, drawing suspicious looks from two women who were passing with a baby in a perambulator and a pug on a leash. He bowed to them and they hurried by. Miss Pierce's feelings about anything—especially the man who had pursued her and to whom, St. John thought, she had not been indifferent at least at one time—were none of his business. He had acted on his conscience, his honor as a gentleman, and his responsibilities as a magistrate, but there the matter ended.

He gazed toward the house in which his betrothed lived, a hundred feet away. He sighed. It felt good to sigh. He wondered if Miss Gretehed would notice if he indulged in it on occasion. He doubted she would mind if she did. She was rather even-tempered about these sorts of things, he thought.

St. John walked the rest of the way to the house, climbed the steps, and put his hand to the knocker. The door was opened by Lady Juno's butler, but by only a very small crack. The butler peeked through it. St. John leaned to the side to regard the man curiously.

"Sir St. John, you are here."

St. John's brows rose.

"Indeed, Mimsley. You are quite right."

The two men stood for a moment contemplating each other through the small opening of the door. St. John cleared his throat.

"May I come in?"

The butler's face was immobile, as was the rest of his body for a long moment. Then he pulled the door open all the way and St. John stepped into the hall.

He heard the row immediately and stood still for a moment in mild surprise. Then, as if nothing at all were unusual, he casually took off his hat and handed it to the butler. Mimsley's face was a mask of apology.

"Do you wish to announce me, Mimsley?" St. John said quite evenly.

The old man looked at him, nodded solemnly, and stepped around Sir Pennworthy. He led the way down the short corridor and to the door to the parlor at the back of the house. The shouting grew louder as they neared it, the cries of a young, distraught female mingled with the screams of an older, rather alarmingly raspy voice.

"They have been at it for almost an hour, sir," the butler said by way of morose explanation, staring at the door before him as if willing it to remain closed. Then he opened it and admitted St. John.

The sound of the baronet's name being said by the butler caused an immediate transformation in the room. Lady Juno, who had been calling her companion a rather distasteful name in a rather sharp voice, closed her mouth instantly upon seeing St. John at the open door. Miss Gretehed's mouth, on the other hand, fell open at sight of Sir Pennworthy, her hand flying to cover it only after a stunned cry had escaped. Then she sat down suddenly in a chair behind her, threw her face into her hands, and began to cry violently.

"Sir St. John," Lady Juno said loudly. "You have arrived at just the right moment."

"Forgive me, madam, if I beg to differ." St. John strode over to where his betrothed sat hunched over her own hands. He said to her in a soft voice, "Miss Gretehed, is there anything I may do for you?"

"She will not understand!" he heard through muffled sobs. Then the lady raised her reddened, tear-stained face, her expression tormented. She did not look at him, but at the woman across the room from her.

"She is a headstrong, foolish old woman, and she will neither heed me nor her doctors. And when I leave, she will die for lack of caring for herself!" She burst into tears again and covered her face with her wet kerchief.

"See how ungrateful she is, Sir St. John?" crackled Lady Juno from across the room, raising a bony finger to point in her companion's direction. "She nags me and lectures me and cossets me to distraction, and I will have it no longer, I tell you! I will have it no longer!"

"It seems, madam, that any person would appreciate such concern for his welfare as Miss Gretehed takes for yours."

He thought his tone was reasonable, as were his words. Lady Juno obviously did not agree.

"You experience her shrew-like devotion for a week or a month, sir, and I dare you to say the same!" she exclaimed.

St. John's brows rose a fraction.

"I hasten to remind you, my lady, that you are speaking of my betrothed," he said evenly.

She cracked a blast of laughter. "Ha! And more the fortune for you, my good man. She will drive you to madness as surely as she has driven me, I tell you, with her medical treatises and her diagnoses and her constant pestering about measurements and schedules. Mark my words!"

St. John came as close to glaring at a lady as he ever had. Instead, he bent his head and touched the companion's shoulder with a gentle hand. She jerked at the touch, and twisted around in her seat to regard him with something akin to dread, St. John was startled to note.

"Oh, sir! You cannot know how I have suffered here!" she cried pitifully, gray eyes brimming with tears. "I have only tried to help, have cared for her to the best of my abilities, have added months to her time, more than any of the doctors expected—"

"At the cost of my ease!" cut in the old woman across the room.

"See how she despises me, when I have been her only comfort!" Miss Gretehed dissolved into tears again. St. John, feeling not altogether steady himself, looked down at her with compassion.

"You are free to leave here this very instant, Miss Gretehed, if you wish it. I shall take you to my sister's and you may live there until we are wed."

He was entirely unprepared for the lady to jump up from her chair, stare at him in a manner not at all conducive to his self-confidence, and begin to shake her head back and forth.

"What are you saying, sir?" she gasped in astonishment. "That I should leave Lady Juno when she is in such a state, so wholly distraught that she knows not what she says to me or to you?" Her gray eyes were filled with disbelief and, St. John thought, disapproval of him. She turned to look across the room at her employer and her expression softened to anxious compassion. "Why, look at her now. She has only come to this because she knows I will leave eventually. She cannot bear to see me go, and she has been frightened into this abnormal passion on account of your anticipated appointment here this afternoon. What reminds her of the day of my ultimate departure sickens her, cannot you see this?"

"You fool!" spat Lady Juno from where she had sunken like a thin, black shadow into a chair at the edge of the room. "*I* arranged for your introduction to the baronet, idiot. I knew he was searching for a wife and it seemed the most expedient way to be rid of you. She has so little sense she did not even recognize that!"

This last was directed at St. John. It seemed Lady Juno was coming to the end of her physical energy, but her tongue was as sharp as ever. He directed a hard look at her, satisfied when her gaze flickered under his, but not significantly. She was glaring again at her companion almost before the moment passed.

Miss Gretehed was crying again, face uncovered except for a hand that she held to her mouth. St. John extended his handkerchief to her. She turned her gaze away from the older woman, looked at the linen square as if it were poisoned, and shrank back from him a step. St.

John put the handkerchief back into his waist-coat pocket.

"I understand your concerns, Miss Gretehed. There is no reason that we must hurry our wedding date. A month or two should suffice to find a suitable replacement for your services, so that you may be comforted that Lady Juno is in caring and capable hands when you finally leave."

"Sir," he heard her say in a wavering voice. "I cannot do it."

"Cannot do what, Miss Gretehed? Postpone our wedding?"

"I cannot leave Lady Juno. Ever."

St. John heard a groan from across the room as he mused on how many times he had heard the words "cannot" and "ever" over the past several months. It seemed quite a bit too many.

"Our marriage should prove to be decidedly difficult to negotiate on a daily basis in that case, ma'am. Lady Juno's estate is at least a hundred miles from mine in Devon, I rather think." St. John lifted his right hand and contemplated the nails on his fingers. He breathed on them and rubbed them against the lapel of his plum-colored coat before looking up again at his one-time betrothed.

"Ha!" Lady Juno cracked. "He is too good for you, Victoria! You have lost him with this idiocy." Her tone was spiteful.

St. John regarded the noblewoman evenly. "My lady, I am a man of my word. Miss Gretehed is yet betrothed to me until she informs me otherwise." He returned his gaze to the companion's. She was looking at him with painful comprehension.

"Sir St. John," she said in a tight voice. "I am honored by your constancy. But I cannot leave my post here with Lady Juno. I cannot marry you, and I wish our engagement to be at an end." She twisted her hands before her in agitation. St. John stepped over to her and took one hand in his. She gave it to him begrudgingly, but he held it gently.

"Would you not like time to consider your decision, madam? I shall not be impatient if you should prefer to think about this at a time when emotions are not running quite so high." He looked at her warmly.

She shook her head. "No, sir, I am quite placid now and certain that I have made the worthy choice." She looked over at the older woman, who sat staring at her companion with something less than affection and closer to what looked like disdain. Miss Gretehead swallowed visibly and then, surprisingly, produced a small but grim smile. "I shall get along very well here," she said to him. "But I thank you for your offer, nonetheless."

St. John nodded, withdrew his hand, and bowed to Miss Gretehed. He stepped away from her and directed his adieu to the two women at once.

"Ladies, I wish you a pleasant sojourn in Bath. Good day to you both." St. John departed then, giving an enigmatic smile to the butler as the old man handed him his hat at the front door. He stepped out into the warm summer evening.

It did not take him long to reach his destination. It was not yet seven o'clock, the late-season sunshine still coming in through the windows at

Brooks's despite the hour. St. John took a seat by a window and ordered a bottle of brandy to be brought to his table. He sat quietly, waiting for the drink. He looked out at a St. James Street thin of both pedestrians and carriages this far into the summer, and contemplated his situation.

Many hours later, if he had been able to recognize where he was and what he was doing, he would have been rather surprised to find himself sitting in a green on a bench across the street from a town house whose knocker was gone and shutters closed for the summertime. A half-empty bottle of heaven knew what rested in his slack hand against the bench seat as he stared at the abandoned house with glassy eyes. Despite the fact that he had come these many blocks with much trouble simply to see this very building, he was too successfully distracted by the vision in his memory to appreciate the view. He was thinking of a pair of eyes—wide, expressive, beautiful. They were not gray, although something in the very far back of his mind told him he must be making some sort of mistake in the color.

For the eyes in his imagination he could not stop pondering were most assuredly hazel.

Fifteen

When St. John awoke, the sun peeking through the cracks between the draperies was high in the sky, or rather low, given that it had already long ago decided to begin its descent for the day. The chamber was warm despite drawn curtains, and he pushed the coverlet off with irritation, still half-asleep, and struggled to discern where he could possibly be. He opened bloodshot eyes to stare at the ceiling above him.

Home, of course, he was home. Where else would he be? Trying to ignore the wretched taste in his mouth and the pounding of his head, he sat up and moved his legs over the side of the bed.

The door to the dressing room opened, and his valet came in, carrying a brass basin and towel, setting them on the dressing table without comment. Then he stepped over to the door and opened it. As St. John watched foggily, Rogers accepted a silver tray from the maid standing in the corridor, who closed the door behind him as he walked over to where St. John sat. He placed the tray on the nightstand beside the baronet's bed. He was obliged to move aside a book to do so: a volume of letters written in an ancient language, marked at his master's place with a slip of notepaper on which was scribed a note in the hand of a Young Lady of Quality. He did so with great care. Then the gentleman's gentleman poured out a cup of steaming coffee, added a healthy quantity of sugar, and put it into the hands of his employer. He straightened, and walked across the room to prepare Sir Pennworthy's shaving gear.

St. John sat for a moment unmoving, feeling the heat of the cup against his palms and fingers. Every inch of him, even his fingertips, felt battered. He raised the cup to his lips and burnt his tongue on the scalding liquid. He did not curse. St. John rarely cursed. Never when he himself was the fool to blame.

"Rogers," he said, sipping again, this time more carefully. "Did I, perchance, make my way home unaccompanied last night?"

"This morning is more accurate, sir," replied his valet, lathering the shaving soap in a small brass dish. "And no, you were in fact accompanied."

"By whom, may I inquire?" The evening was beginning to come back to him very slowly, in pathetic detail.

"By a charley, sir," the valet said without a trace of emotion in his voice. "He found you sitting in a park, quite alone, and feared for your safety."

St. John recalled, very vaguely, something of the watch's arrival. He had been, he thought now, reciting poetry. No. It was impossible. Well, not quite.

"My safety? Was I in danger?" He felt no shame questioning his valet in such a manner. Rogers had been with him for many years, had known him since he was barely a lad. Sir Pennworthy was not a tea-nipper, but never before had Rogers met his master on the doorstep at dawn three sheets to the wind and escorted by the watch. But there was a first time for everything.

"No, sir. You were sitting quite peaceably, the man reported, on a bench in Abbey Street." The valet regarded him blandly. "You seemed quite comfortable there, according to the charley, but he thought it better to make certain you reached home without mishap, as you had no companions about you and the streets were rather deserted at that hour." Rogers extended the towel in indication that the shaving materials were ready for his master.

Placing his cup on the nightstand with exaggerated care, St. John stood rather shakily and walked over to the dressing table. Rogers handed him his dressing robe, and St. John shrugged into it, sat himself down before the table, and leaned his head back. The valet placed a towel around Sir Pennworthy's neck, spread shaving soap on his master's cheeks and jaw, and set the razor to the man's skin. After a minute during which they both remained silent, one shaving, the other being shaved, the valet spoke again. His voice was completely neutral.

"Sir, as it appears that your betrothal is at an end, and you are now honorably free to amuse yourself as you wish, might I suggest that you make a visit to Randall Street before too long?"

St. John Pennworthy was not a blushing man.

Nonetheless, he was glad of the shaving foam that obscured his face at that moment.

"Rogers, you are out of line." His voice was stern.

"Yes, sir," the valet said. "Please forgive my presumption."

St. John sat while his valet finished shaving him, thinking on Rogers's probably very wise suggestion. It had been a very long time since St. John had partaken of the particular kind of companionship that was available on Randall Street— or at least had once been available there. St. John could barely remember the last time he had been with a woman, it had been so long ago. Perhaps a year, perhaps two? There had been that young widow in Leeds when he had been in the region investigating fabric mills. She had been lovely, and warm, and very discreet.

The valet wiped his master's jaw clean of soap and St. John stood up and immersed his face in the bowl of clear warm water. After a long moment he drew it out slowly, watching the droplets of milky water drip from his brows, nose, and chin as those parts of his face emerged. He straightened, dried his face with a towel, and ran his fingers through his hair to distribute the remnants of droplets that clung to the gold locks at the edges of his face. He accepted the shirt and trousers Rogers placed in his hands and walked into the dressing room.

It had been a pleasure with her, but not enough of one. He removed his dressing gown and nightshirt and pulled his arms into the linen shirt, buttoning it slowly with fingers that were finally beginning to feel the way they had the previous afternoon. Coffee did wonders for a man. He stepped into his trousers and fastened them. She had told him afterward that she had enjoyed herself but that she was looking for a husband again. There was nothing like sharing this particular pleasure with someone you loved, she had said. They had parted amicably at the end of his business in the region, St. John because he had not been the same two years ago as he was now, and she because he had not been the one she was looking for in the end.

Rogers entered the room in time to assist his master in donning his fashionably snug blue kerseymere coat. He inspected the job St. John had made of his cravat, and then handed the baronet a tall-crowned hat. St. John took it and set it atop his head.

"Thank you, Rogers. You have been quite a help to me this afternoon. I am grateful for it."

The valet, whose duty it was to shave, dress, and otherwise care for his master's person, bowed slightly, knowing what the other man was not saying with his words.

St. John turned, went down the stairs, and ordered his curricle to be brought around. When he ascended the box of the vehicle and his tiger asked him where they were headed, he responded without so much as a twitch of his lips that they were going to Randall Street.

"St. John, love! What a marvelous surprise. It has been an age since I have had the pleasure of seeing your handsome face in my drawing room."

St. John had been admitted to the woman's house via a back door. He stood now in an upstairs parlor; the lady who had spoken was stretched out upon a chaise and dressed in an extraordinarily flattering violet-colored gown clearly meant to be worn only inside the house. Her luxuriant black hair was unbound and cascaded around her bared shoulders. In her hand was a book, which she had closed upon his entrance into the room. She extended her other hand for him and St. John took it and raised it to his lips.

"How are you, Clara?" He took the elegant Chippendale chair that she gestured to next to the chaise.

"I am as well as can be. And you, St. John? I have heard you are now a baronet." Her violet eyes assessed him appreciatively from behind dark lashes. "How very wonderful for you."

St. John smiled slightly, thinking how age had only improved the good looks of Clara Dougherty. He had seen her at a distance many times during the past several years—at the opera, the Park—but never this close up, and now he saw that she had changed. She had been an attractive slip of a girl when he had first met her that night in the Green Room after the play. Now she was a mature woman, seven years older, and seven years more confident and experienced.

"I am indeed a baronet now. How did you discover it?"

The dark beauty laughed throatily.

"I discover everything, love. It is all I have to do, after all, but sit here and learn what it is my betters are doing out there in the world." There was a flash in her dark eyes as she spoke, and St. John remembered what had first attracted him to her in the theater that night. She, like he, had not been born into particular wealth or power. But Clara had wanted from an early age to make something of herself, and had not stopped until she had achieved it. But she knew, and had probably known for long, that as the mistress of a duke, she had already reached the pinnacle of her success.

"Betters in no meaningful way," St. John murmured. He glanced at the book in her lap. "What is it you are reading, Clara? Not still those romances you so loved?"

She smiled, red-tinted lips curving into a satisfied grin.

"When I have the notion. But I read a number of other things now as well, St. John." She glanced down at the slim volume in her lap. "This is poetry, if you must know."

She also read history, on occasion, and books on art and music. The men she entertained now—and entertained in the strictest sense, those who came for dinner and conversation only as guests of His Grace—did not necessarily expect a courtesan to provide an intellectually elevated atmosphere, but Clara Dougherty was happy to surprise them. So was her duke. He, however, had not been the one to first encourage her in improving herself. The inspiration had come from a Christmas present received in the mail from Devon six years ago. It had been a book profiling the lives of several great historical women.

She looked up now at St. John Pennworthy and

smiled. He smiled back and she was tempted to blush under the influence of that unnerving sapphire regard.

"Clara, I have come to make you a proposal," he said. St. John held his hand up. "It is not an offer to win you back from Dumfries," he said quickly before she could protest. Her expression was surprised but not unduly so. St. John supposed she received offers of one sort or another on a regular basis. "Not in the strictest sense, that is.

"I seek a wife," he continued without hesitation. "You and I have done well together in the past, and I believe we could do as well together in the future. In short, I propose to you marriage."

Now she was surprised. St. John watched as the woman across from him made herself clearly understand what it was she had heard him say. He sat waiting patiently. He was becoming quite the dab hand at knowing what to expect in this situation. But why did they all seem so befuddled? He considered her while he waited.

She was well educated for one of her profession, well spoken and not above thirty yet. Their alliance of seven years ago had been brief, their break amicable. She had been his first such relationship, and when he had soon discovered that transient pleasure-taking was not for him, he had given her up to a wealthy earl who was eager to take care of the lovely courtesan himself. He knew that she'd had a few other protectors before the duke stepped in to make her his offer. That had been two years ago.

Clara took a deep breath and finally opened

her mouth to speak. He was not a vain or proud man, but still her response was somewhat unexpected. St. John would have liked to say it was her tone of voice that caught him off guard, but he had to admit it was really the words rather than how they were spoken that disjointed him.

"St. John, love," she said, a slow smile crossing her lips, "now what would I want to go and get married for, when I have my dear Lord Dumfries to keep me comfortable and happy?" Clara's long, black lashes batted coquettishly against her cheeks as she gestured around her at the opulently furnished apartment. It was true, the place was rather grand, and she did look quite at home and contented in it. But had not a chum once told him that all Birds of Paradise wanted to settle down someday, before their charms paled and they lost their protectors to younger women?

St. John had not believed it much then. Seeing the satisfaction in his former paramour's eyes, he was more certain of its falseness now.

"You could have a household of your own, much larger than this one, Clara. A house in Town and two in the country," he said, the enthusiasm for this exchange already beginning to slip away from him with the passing moments.

She smiled again, and St. John was struck with the idea that this woman was of a certainty mistress of herself and of her future.

"I already have a house in London: this one," she said, looking indeed quite the duchess in her decadent surroundings. "His Grace has signed over the place to me. And, at the sake of hurting your feelings, love, why would I ever want to have a house in the country? So I could molder away forgotten there like the little women you and yours call wives?" Her smile wavered a bit, but then she picked up a feather fan on the small table beside her and began to wave it languidly beneath her chin. St. John's gaze was drawn to where the feathers whispered against her deeply cleaved bosom, barely concealed by the violet fabric. This seemed to give her confidence and she added unhurriedly, "Dumfries is very generous, St. John."

"I am also generous, Clara." St. John could not bear to let it go, although he knew he would, finally. He quite suddenly realized he had no heart for it.

"You?" she looked surprised. She extended her bared arm to him. "Do you see this lovely thing? His Grace gave it to me just last week, for my birthday." She twisted her arm and in the midday light peeking through the corners of the drawn window curtains, St. John had ample opportunity to appreciate the luxurious richness of the gold, ruby, and emerald bracelet adorning Clara's narrow wrist.

"Isn't it lovely?" she cooed. Her voice sounded odd to him.

"Lovely." He looked away from the vulgar piece. "I gave you jewelry." He noted this for posterity's sake.

She shrugged. "Ha!"

"I did!" He did not like to insist with a lady, but then Clara was not precisely a lady, as it were, although he had always before unfailingly treated her as one. But his pride was pricked a little. Dumfries was an old lecher.

"Once!" she retorted quickly. So, she did remember.

"It was a beautiful thing, as I recall."

"Colorless," she countered. "I like colors. Simply adore them."

St. John glanced quickly around the opulently furnished room. "Indeed." He stood, Clara's eyes going with him as he seemed to shake his broad shoulders into decision.

"Well, my dear, it has been a great pleasure seeing you again. I regret that we cannot come to an agreement." He said this with a rare lack of sincerity of feeling. He realized that this had perhaps not been the best choice of a bride among his many choices, and that he had been fortunate in her refusal. "So I shall be going now."

"But you have only just arrived, love," the beauty protested graciously, extending her hand for him to take. He did, and bowed over it. She had meant him to kiss it, they both knew. "I don't suppose you will come back again sometime when His Grace is out of Town?" Her words were at once sultry and light, promising. St. John felt like sighing.

"I shan't, Clara. I seek a bride, and none other. But I thank you for the time you have generously given me on this occasion." St. John turned and made his way out of the chamber and into the hall, where he gathered his hat and let the footman see him out the back door.

Clara Dougherty gazed after him with regret. She *was* fond of him, had been since he had taken her out of that twopenny theater where she was getting nothing but heartache for the favors demanded of her by manager and theatergoers alike; he had made of her a high-class courtesan. He had even taught her how to eat at table like a lady. St. John Pennworthy had been the kindest protector she had ever had, even after they had parted. And certainly the most handsome.

Not the most wise where it came to his own good, however.

Clara gazed down unseeing at the gaudy jewels on her arm; then she sat up and reached over to the table beside her where there rested a small enameled box. With painted fingertips she drew a minuscule key out from under it to open the tiny lid of the box, and withdrew from the velvet-lined interior a delicate, sparkling bracelet.

The gold-work was so fine and the diamonds on the piece were so bright that Clara was afraid to wear it for fear it might jinx her. But she kept it in her little box for the future, when someday she should give it to her daughter, a daughter being raised in the country by gentry to be a real lady. Someday Margaret would marry a fine gentleman like St. John Pennworthy—a great-grandson of an earl for all that he was a Cit—and she would wear the bracelet on her own wedding day. The bracelet was, after all, a piece for one better than Clara herself was or would ever be.

St. John left Town the next day, telling his servants that he would meet them in Somerset at the home of his parents. Then he rode off without a word as to where he was going. His servants did not believe he was preceding them to Somerset, but nonetheless followed his orders and thought not another thing about it.

St. John was going out for a ride, that was all. He took a saddle pack of clean shirts and small-clothes, shaving gear, and a pistol, and he set out on the Great North Road. He was not on it for long before he turned off onto a smaller toll road, and then from there onto an even smaller country road that led into hamlets and tiny villages along the way. Occasionally he crossed a field or rode through a wood if there was a path.

He stopped the first night at an inn. The taproom was filled with working men and farmers. St. John found himself a corner alone and sipped an ale brought to him by a comely serving girl. She winked at him when she set his second tankard on the table. Six hours later, having spoken with no one since he walked into the place, he left the serving girl happily satisfied and asleep in the room he had paid for on the upper floor and went out to the stables in the dark of the predawn morning.

The second day he rode until early afternoon. As the sun began to dip from its apex ever so slowly into the west, St. John stretched out in a field and fell asleep. When he woke it was evening and he was hungry. Brushing himself off, he mounted his horse again and set off for the nearest village. An old, retired curate took him in that night, proving to be more interested in the news St. John had to share with him about his years in India than where he had come from the day before. The old man never questioned why a gentleman of his stamp was traveling with only a horse and a pistol as companions. St. John bid him adieu the next morning, after sunrise this time, and rode off into the already warm summer day.

Three and a half weeks after leaving London, Sir St. John Pennworthy appeared at his parents' home, his face tanned and the expression in his eyes inscrutable. He washed and dressed in clean clothes and went to the parlor to meet his family. His father greeted him warmly and his step-mother embraced him before his half sisters hurried into the room and threw themselves into his arms. He laughed, teased them, and let them tell him all about how they had been passing their time in the month since they had seen each other in Town.

It was only moments, therefore, before he heard once more of the house party that his aunt had planned for Stratford-upon-Avon. The family would be removing to Lady Fitzwarren's two days hence, and, now that he was home, St. John was expected to attend with them. Lilly told him in an aside as they walked in to dinner how very glad she was that he had returned in time to accompany them to their aunt's. On the same breath she let him know in no uncertain terms how likewise pleased she was that his engagement with Miss Gretehed had come to naught. St. John, who had never announced the betrothal to his family, ignored the comment as he deposited his sister at her seat at the table.

That night, alone in his room after having told Rogers that they would be leaving for his aunt's home with the family in two days' time, St. John drew out a slim, leather-bound volume. It came from the traveling pack whose emptying he had told his valet he would see to himself. He opened it up to the marker and placed the piece of notepaper on the bedstead. His eyes sought the Latin text on the open page of the book, and he smiled slowly, translating as he read aloud the words of the ancient Roman philosopher Seneca softly to himself:

> *Are you surprised, as if it were a novelty, that after such long travel and so many changes of scene you have not been able to shake off the gloom and heaviness of your mind? You need a change of soul rather than a change of climate.*

He laughed ruefully, and then picked up the piece of notepaper that served as his marker and went to insert it back into the book. Instead, his fingers unfolded the paper, and St. John stared at the banal words of apology written on the white sheet as if they were old, dear friends.

Sixteen

Alethea stepped down from the carriage and set her foot on the drive in front of Lady Fitzwarren's house. Her sister was already rushing up the steps to the front door as if she hadn't a stitch of breeding.

"Octavia, dear, do behave yourself," Alethea heard her mother say from behind her as Mr. and Mrs. Pierce climbed out of the traveling chaise and joined her on the drive.

The house before them was a gracious Tudor, of well-proportioned red brick and stone. The countess had inherited it from her mother. When Lord Fitzwarren died and his cousin inherited the title and lands, Lady Fitzwarren had retired to the banks of the Avon, refusing to marry again and growing more eccentric and ever plumper as the years went by. Every year she still traveled to London for the Little Season and the Season, but this was the first year in many she had planned a gathering at her home in the country. Her letters had said there would be upwards of thirty guests present, including the girls not yet officially out of the schoolroom. By these Lady

Fitzwarren meant Octavia and the Pennworthy sisters, Lilly and Esther.

As Alethea entered the house, she was met with the enthusiastic welcomes of these young ladies, who had accompanied their aunt into the hall to greet the new arrivals. As she received a kiss on each cheek from Lady Fitzwarren, she restrained herself from looking with too much interest around the large, well-appointed hall. It mattered not that the Misses Pennworthy were already in house, of course. . . .

Alethea's gaze met the gentleman's across the hall and her eyes widened in surprise. He was standing on a lower step of the grand staircase that led up into the second story, looking upon the crowded scene of greetings with benignity. He seemed to see her at just the moment she looked at him, and he smiled in greeting. Alethea felt her cheeks grow warm and was glad of the bonnet she had not yet shed, behind which she turned to shield her blush.

My, but he had grown more handsome yet during the past month! Alethea stole another glance at Sir Pennworthy. His short blond locks were light with sun, but otherwise there was no other obvious change in him. Perhaps it was only the surprise of seeing him here unexpectedly when she had thought not to. When she had hoped to.

Lady Fitzwarren ushered her guests up the stairs and to the apartments and chambers made ready for them. When Alethea passed Sir Pennworthy on the broad step, he held out his hand to her and she paused to shake it.

"Precisely the color I imagined," he said, holding her hand firmly but as if he had forgotten it. His tone of satisfaction and the unanticipated words brought Alethea up short out of her fantasy-like musings.

"I beg your pardon, sir?"

Sir Pennworthy's brows lifted as if in surprise at her question.

"Why, your rose, Miss Pierce. This shade suits you so well. Much better than yellow, I dare say." It seemed so very obvious to him, apparently, but it took Alethea a moment to recall that she wore a single fresh rose pinned to the bodice of her traveling gown. She had picked it from a bush in full bloom near the inn they had stopped at earlier in the day for refreshment; as Alethea's hand went to the deep red flower, she imagined it must be quite wilted by this time. But the baronet seemed not to mind. He stared at her with obvious contentment and Alethea could only smile in response.

"I thank you, Sir St. John."

With her smile his thoughts seemed to shift, and he took her hand again and shook it as if he had not already done so.

"It is a great pleasure to see you again. I hope you are well." His voice was low and pleasing. Alethea was not surprised to find it quite pleasing to hear again. She withdrew her hand from his for a second time.

"Thank you, sir, I am well. Your aunt is kind to include us in her party this month."

He grinned. "Even if my aunt had not already grown fond of your family, Miss Pierce, Lilly and Esther would have had it no other way. They have felt the lack of your sister quite acutely since

London." He regarded her warmly, an odd look in his eyes, and Alethea felt tingling in the hand she had just reclaimed. She nodded and then was swept up the stairs to the guest chambers along with the rest of her family.

Two hours later, having rested and washed and changed for dinner, Alethea met Lord and Lady Bramfield descending the stairs on their way to the drawing room. They greeted each other happily and made their way to the drawing room where the party was gathering before dinner.

"Aha! Miss Pierce," Lady Fitzwarren beckoned to Alethea as she entered. There were more than a dozen people present, and Alethea made her way over to her hostess, exchanging pleasantries with others as she went.

"Lady Fitzwarren, the accommodations you have given me are quite lovely. Thank you very much."

"Nonsense, child, you are welcome here as would be my own niece—or daughter, or what have you," the countess said bracingly.

Nonplused, Alethea did not let her reaction show on her face. She turned instead to greet Lord and Lady Fredericks, who had just entered and were headed toward them.

"Dearest Miss Pierce, how good it is to see you again so soon," Lady Fredericks bussed her on the cheek. "And how glad we were to hear the news from London yesterday regarding that contemptible Fenton."

Alethea's brow furrowed.

"We have been on the road, ma'am, and have not heard anything from London since several days ago," she said, hoping her countenance did not reveal the anxiety roused in her at the mention of Bertram Fenton's name. Her father had overheard Lady Fredericks's comment, and stepped up to their little group to inquire.

"What have you learned, my lady? Has that rascal returned to Town after all of these weeks?" His voice was concerned, sober, and Alethea knew he was thinking that someday he might still have to fight the man.

"Oh, no, Mr. Pierce. It appears that he is quite gone for good, actually." Lady Fredericks turned to her husband for confirmation, and Lord Fredericks nodded.

"Gone? What do you mean, gone?" Mr. Pierce asked.

"We could barely believe it when we heard it, but it seems he has been transported to Australia."

"Australia!" Alethea felt her face drain of color. "Whatever for, Lady Fredericks?"

"Yes, Hecuba. Do tell." Lady Fitzwarren said smoothly. She was watching Miss Pierce's face with avid concentration, but she glanced away to look at her nephew. Sir Pennworthy had just entered the room, and as the attention of the dozen or so guests there had been taken by Lady Fredericks's astounding news, he turned his gaze, too. He seemed to avoid Lady Fitzwarren's gaze quite carefully, that lady was interested to note.

"Fredericks, you heard it at your club," Lady Fredericks said to her husband. "It's best you tell the story."

"Well, the details aren't much, just some scraps garnered from several different sources," Lord Fredericks explained apologetically. "Word has it, though, that Fenton was discovered to have been the culprit in the untimely death of those two girls in Exmouth a couple of years back."

Gasps and exclamations erupted from the group assembled.

"He is a *murderer?*" Mr. Pierce's voice was hardened with shock. "The blackguard! I w—"

"Papa," Alethea said quickly, putting a restraining hand on her father's arm. Her face was white but composed. "Tell us the rest, please, Lord Fredericks. How was this discovered?"

"Seems the Runners have been investigating on behalf of the village where it occurred for two years now, but to no good. Put a little money in the broth pot, though, and you're bound to come up with new soup, I always say." The older man looked around knowingly and nodded.

"What my husband means to say is that it appears an anonymous gentleman seems to have encouraged Bow Street to extend its investigation farther than it might otherwise have searched. When the Runner reported what he had found regarding Mr. Fenton the other day, it revealed not only theft and fraud but also murder." Lady Fredericks turned compassionate eyes on Alethea, and then looked back at the rest of her listeners. "For what it is worth, the deaths of those two girls seem not to have been premeditated. In any case, Fenton is suffering for them now."

"Transportation is too good for him!" Mr. Pierce insisted. "The villain should have hanged."

"Bow Street—and the unnamed patron—were apparently concerned that due to Mr. Fenton's connections he would somehow escape execution

if brought to Newgate," Lady Fredericks continued. "I believe the news was that he would be
making a lifetime's career in the copper mines,
instead."

There were murmurs all about the room as this
remarkable news was mused over, discussed, and
dissected. It proved to be the topic of dinner conversation; unpleasant as it was, it was by far the
most exciting thing that had happened to London Society in months, and the principals—except, of course, the poor girls and Fenton
himself—were present, to boot. Lady Fitzwarren
prided herself on the discretion of her intimates,
however, and at Alethea's end of the dinner table
speculation was rather more general and philo-
sophical than pointed.

Several hours later, Alethea climbed the grand
staircase and found her way to her bedchamber
pensively and not without a certain trembling in
her limbs. The news was astounding, unsettling,
and somehow oddly, awfully satisfying.

She felt wholly wretched. How could she have
once believed she loved a man who had done
such a frightful thing? It was too dreadful to
think about. She had thought he was simply a
rake, but this . . . this was terrible!

And to imagine his punishment. . . . It sent
shivers of terror up her spine entertaining the
notion. Alethea had heard plenty of stories of
how the mines were worked in Australia. The
men in those mines in her imagination did not
have charming smiles, liquid brown eyes, and
devastatingly elegant waistcoats. How would Bertram Fenton survive in such a place? She shiv-

ered again in the oppressive warmth of her room.

Alethea went to the window and pulled back the draperies. The air was warm, not appreciably better than inside the room, but there was a tiny breeze that stirred the locks of hair falling in front of her eyes. She brushed them back and gazed out at the hazy, starlit night.

Had she imagined the look that had passed from Lord Bramfield to Sir Pennworthy when Lady Fredericks spoke the words "anonymous gentleman" this evening in the drawing room? Somehow Alethea had found her gaze drawn to the blond man as Lord and Lady Fredericks were speaking; then she had caught Timothy's sideways glance toward that gentleman when everyone else's attention had been glued to what was being revealed. Sir Pennworthy's expression had remained completely neutral.

Alethea had looked to the baronet because of the secrets they shared, not able to resist seeing his response to the news of Mr. Fenton's transportation. After all, Sir Pennworthy had, without being asked, acted her champion several times even before her own father had known of Fenton's inappropriate attachment to her. On those occasions, the baronet had acted out of a code of honor that seemed as integral to him as breathing. Had he, could he have, acted thus again? Somehow, despite how incredible it seemed, Alethea could not doubt it.

The next day heavy rain kept the party indoors, reading, playing billiards and cards, and gossiping about the news—the accounts of Bertram Fenton's crime and exile not being the least, of course—that each party had brought from their respective places in the country. The remainder of the guests arrived, waterlogged and mud-spattered, happy to not have become irretrievably stuck on the muddy roads.

Alethea did not manage to speak with Sir Pennworthy privately the entire day. She found herself in his company more than once, however; first playing pin the tail on the rabbit with their sisters and several others in the drawing room after nuncheon, and again later in the library when he surprised her there reading.

He entered the room, and then seemed to be brought up short when he spotted her sitting in a deep leather chair with her feet tucked up underneath her and a book in her lap. She had not been precisely reading—mostly thinking. His gaze seemed questioning, and he did not say anything for a moment as she looked across the room to him above her spectacles and fumbled with the book in her lap. Then two other guests came into the library to play a game of chess on the table set up near the broad bay window. Sir Pennworthy conversed with them together with Alethea for a moment before he found the journal he was looking for. Then he quit the room rather quickly, she thought.

Alethea slept badly in the heat that night.

The following day dawned bright and clear, but still warmer yet, no relief from the unusual heat having come from the torrents of the previous day. The ground was tested for muddiness; when it passed muster as sufficiently firm it was de-

cided that the party should make a foray to the
ruins of the medieval abbey situated not a mile
away from Lady Fitzwarren's house. A picnic was
packed and sent ahead to the abbey in carriages,
while the countess's guests walked the short distance at a leisurely pace, enjoying the scenery of
the gentle wood-scattered countryside as they
strolled.

It was some distance into the walk that Alethea
paused to study a cluster of unusual wildflowers
blooming off the path. The group had spread
out considerably, and she told her companions
to continue along without her. She assured them
she would take up with whichever person came
along next. Lord Bramfield, engaged in a cheer-
ful argument with Toby Wisterly, continued along
the path, and his wife followed quietly after,
glancing back at Alethea and smiling when she
saw who would shortly meet her friend on the
way. Alethea was just putting the final strokes to
a drawing she was making in her tiny sketchbook
when she was surprised by the voice of Sir
Pennworthy, who had followed her off the path
and into the tall grass.

" 'And please the better from a pensive face,
a thoughtful eye, and a reflecting brow.' What is
it that you are contemplating, Miss Pierce?"

Alethea turned, readying herself with a deep
breath and a smile on her lips.

"Perhaps you should call me Miss Kelly, sir?"
she responded, calling quickly to mind the ad-
dressee of the poem he had quoted in order to
quell her suddenly jumping nerves. "I am studying these wildflowers. They are quite unusual in

both shape and texture. I do not believe I have ever seen them before."

The gentleman looked over her shoulder at the drawing in her hand, and his brows rose.

"A species peculiar to the Avon, do you suppose?" the baronet mused. "A superb likeness, Miss Kelly—ah, Miss Pierce. You are an artist."

"Nonsense, sir. I only dabble at what I enjoy." Alethea slid sketchbook, pencil, and spectacles into her reticule, bending her head to hide her pleasure at Sir Pennworthy's compliment. Why had not Monsieur Le Maine's flatteries ever made her pulse quicken the way this man's slightest notice did? Probably because the Frenchman's attention had not been shared with anyone else and therefore felt less precious. *Alethea, you are a contrary dolt,* she scolded herself. She began to walk back to the path, Sir Pennworthy at her side.

"Do you enjoy poetry, ma'am? I am impressed with your recognition of Mr. Lamb's sonnet." His voice was neutral, always so neutral. Alethea wondered how the baronet managed to present himself so evenly when she was certain her own emotions were as clear as the day in her voice.

"Why should I not know the work, Sir St. John? You do."

She heard Sir Pennworthy chuckle and glanced up at him briefly. They were at a bend in the path, and no others were in sight as they retook the pathway and began to once again walk toward the ruins. Alethea had spoken quickly to mask her nerves. She was glad he responded so good-naturedly to her taunt.

"*Touché*, Miss Pierce. And the work of the ancients, is that something you likewise dabble in about which I must also not experience a sensation of wonder?"

This time Alethea chuckled.

"No, sir, you are rightly justified in your surprise on that account," she responded. "But that too is more unremarkable than one would think. My governess was a frustrated lady-scholar, and taught us Latin as well as a little Greek when my mother was not attending. She used Master Seneca's letters, of which moral ruminations she was rather fond, to give us our lessons. As well as a bit of poetry."

"Poetry?"

"Yes. Ovid, in particular."

"Ovid? What? The *Metamorphoses?*"

Alethea bit her lip, repressing a twitching that augured ill for her composure.

"The *Amores,* I fear."

"The *Amores!* I am shocked." He looked down at her, a grin playing at the corners of his beautiful mouth. Alethea swallowed roughly. "Thoroughly unsuitable for a maiden's schoolroom, I should say. And not at all in line with your governess' interest in Seneca, either," he added curiously. It was clear that he was not at all offended.

"Indeed, Sir St. John," she responded, dimpling now out of mirth rather than embarrassment. "My governess was a peculiar sort. In any case, when my parents discovered the evil she was perpetrating she was turned off without the slightest notice and without a reference. She is now languishing in a house for fallen women; I believe they call it the *Edinburgh Review.* My parents always feared as much. I send her half of my allowance every quarter, in gratitude and pity, of course." She glanced up at him again from beneath lowered lashes and saw him nod sensibly, brows furrowed in an expression of such serious contemplation that she knew now, knowing him better, was affected in fun. Suppressing her giggles with great effort, she watched as a smile now crossed his handsome face. Alethea felt her heart turn over in her breast.

"I commend you, madam, on your learning and compassion both." His voice was not what Alethea expected when he said these words, and suddenly a start of discomfort ran through her.

"Sir, I must apologize to you very belatedly in lieu of not being able to make my apology in person to the appropriate recipient," she said rather quickly. The gentleman walking beside her looked down at her in curious interest. Alethea folded her hands before her.

"I did not mean at all to discommode Miss Gretehed when I so rudely interrupted your conversation those weeks ago at Lady Juno's house. Do you recall it?" She glanced up fretfully. "Of course you do, how foolish of me. I assure you, however, that I felt the most wretched thing alive for having put her on the spot like that. Listening to her speak on Hippocrates, I did not imagine she would not be conversant in the Romans as well as the Greeks. It did not occur to me one might learn Greek and not learn Latin, you see. I am afraid I appeared to you both rather forward and quite set up in my own conceit."

Alethea felt relief for having uttered the words she had been stewing over for so many weeks. If

Sir Pennworthy were going to marry the lady, then Alethea wanted him at least to believe she did not think herself better than his wife. How could she be, when Miss Gretehed had had the excellent sense to *accept* his proposal?

The gentleman gazed down at her thoughtfully.

"Your concern reveals the sincerity of your feelings, Miss Pierce. I assure you, if I may be so bold, that it was but a moment's notice to the lady and no more."

Alethea should have felt relief at having discharged her burden and having received such a temperate answer in response. She did not. She felt instead rather dispirited.

"How do Lady Juno and Miss Gretehed go on lately, sir? Have they removed to Bath as intended?" She could not help herself from asking; it felt bittersweet to direct the question to him.

"I expect so, Miss Pierce, but know not," he responded easily, hands clasped behind his back as he walked. "I departed Town over a month ago and have not had news of those ladies since I left there."

Alethea's head came up quickly and she met a surprisingly direct gaze that held hers for a long, informative moment. Finally, in confusion, she looked away and down to her clasped hands. They walked along in silence for another few minutes—both peculiarly short of breath for such a sedate stroll—until they came in sight of the ruins, where members of the party were already gathered in little clusters conversing.

As they approached their friends, the private smiles that played about both their mouths did not go unnoticed by at least two members of the waiting party. Satisfied, Lady Fitzwarren turned to meet the gaze of her elder niece. Lilly Pennworthy winked, stretched out her hand for Octavia Pierce's, and turned to walk into the crumbling ruins.

Seventeen

Alethea lay in bed restlessly, the coverlet crushed at her feet and her brow feeling alarmingly warm to her hand pressed upon it.

The heat was unbearable. It had grown warmer and warmer as the day progressed, and not even the bathe in the tiny lake in the woods—which the gentlemen and ladies had enjoyed separately that day—had served to lessen the misery of the unusually scorching summer weather. All of them were still enjoying themselves, however. The company was lively, amusements after a week at Lady Fitzwarren's home still fresh, and the pleasure of spending the summer together with others away from home significant enough to maintain the general level of satisfaction among the assembled guests.

But this day had been the worst yet, and lack of sleep due to the heat was affecting not only the elder guests after several days. Lady Fitzwarren provided her guests with fans and lemonade and cool corners of her house in which to hide during the more unendurable hours of the afternoon. The weather would alter for the better soon, any hour now, the countess comforted with assurance as the guests departed the drawing room that night after dinner for the private heat of their own rooms. If the storm clouds on the horizon this evening were anything to judge by, the heat would break before too long. Waiting, though, was near agony.

Alethea rose from the discomfort of her damp sheets and went to the window of her small yet beautifully appointed chamber. The windows were thrown open to admit the slightest of breezes, but not a breath stirred in the night air. She could hear the crickets' song, smell the heavy perfume of roses rising from the garden below, and see the unyielding thunderheads rolling down from the north but still miles away yet, obscuring the star-filled sky as they advanced.

She leaned against the window box. She was usually made of heartier stuff, she thought in frustration. Of course, it was not so much her body that was overheated—although it was plenty warm—but her imagination. She could simply not stop thinking of St. John Pennworthy, and it was driving her to distraction.

They had spoken again on several occasions since their walk together to the ruined abbey. But it seemed to Alethea that after that conversation he had somehow withdrawn from her. It was ridiculous to think it, naturally. A gentleman like Sir Pennworthy behaved as a gentleman should under all circumstances. It was her girlish fantasies that imbued that one exchange with any significance as they had in London the night of the Wentworth musicale. He continued to be pleasant company when she had the advantage of it; she could find no fault in his behavior toward her except that he had not appeared overly anxious to be in her presence.

Alethea put her hand to her forehead. She felt fevered. She knew it was the weather, the heat that penetrated every bone in her body; but still she felt as if it were some kind of a punishment for her lack of sense this past week. Why, she was growing so scatter-brained she could barely recognize herself. No gentleman was worth that kind of distraction, especially an inconsistent one, she thought with a little stamp of her foot to emphasize the idea her mind considered. She chuckled at her thespian movement, and ran a palm across her brow again. The heat was much more of an irritation than any man could ever be. And at least there was something a girl could do about the former if she wished.

Alethea pushed herself away from the window and picked up the light summer wrapper lying on the trunk at the end of her bed. She drew the delicate pale green silk on over her chemise, which was all she could bear wearing in the heat of the night, and fastened it at the breast. It was all she had, aside from her long-sleeved night-shift. It would have to do for her little errand. In any case, no one would be around at this hour, not many hours from dawn already.

She was grateful her abigail was sleeping up-stairs with the other maids as she slipped out of her chamber and into the corridor, closing the door softly behind her. Alethea stole down the corridor, making no noise at all in her bared feet, feeling with extraordinary pleasure the texture of the floorboards and thick woven carpets along the narrow way. It felt deliciously like an adventure—going about clad only in her night rail in the middle of the sweltering dark! Stifling a giggle, she took up a candle sitting on a side table in the corridor and lit it handily.

Turning again toward the back of the house, she searched the walls until she found the door for which she was looking and passed quickly through it. It was a servant's stair and Alethea was certain it must lead to the nether regions of the house. She made her way through its narrow darkness and down with ginger steps, heart pounding in her chest as she went. When she reached the bottom, she found that the corridor turned left and right. Orienting herself to the house, Alethea took the right-hand passageway and walked along slowly, feeling with her marvelously free toes dust and the occasional mouse dropping, which made her feel like giggling again. The corridor came to an end finally at a door, and Alethea extinguished her candle, turned the knob with her free hand, and opened the door a minute crack.

There was no light beyond, but as her eyes became accustomed to the darkness, she could see the glinting of brass in several places reflecting the moonlight that came in the windows to the right. The kitchen. Alethea was certain of it. And it was uninhabited. She pushed the door open fully and moved out into the dark, empty space. Stepping over to the hearth, she searched for a moment before her hands landed on the match canister, and she took a stick and struck it to light her candle anew. Satisfied, Alethea went about the room, lighting the candles she found. They were few but set up a pleasant glow in the room hung all about with brass and copper kettles and pans. Then she turned to the icebox.

It was a new addition to the kitchens, Lady Fitzwarren had told them earlier, an armoire-sized cabinet that could maintain a cool temperature rather nicely even on the warmest of days if one stocked it well from the ice cellar out by the stables. Alethea had learned that there were chilled hothouse oranges stored in the box, prepared for supper tonight but abandoned when it was discovered that the strawberries the girls had gathered on their way home from the lake were preferred by the countess's guests instead. Alethea eyed the box and its hidden treasures with glee, wishing she were not alone to experience this forbidden moment of decadent mischief. Belinda would be green with envy when she told her about it on the morrow.

There was something marvelous about creeping around the kitchens alone in the semi-dark in her shift and bared feet. It made Alethea feel deliciously scandalous and totally innocent at one and the same time. A house full of people, she thought as she opened the box and quickly drew forth a wonderfully cold orange, and no one the wiser for her daring. Perhaps one never stopped feeling like a girl inside, even when the experiences she had and lessons she'd learned made her feel sometimes as if she had lived three lifetimes already. Alethea turned to move to the table and sit, and almost jumped out of her skin.

A man stood across the room from her in the wavering light.

"Sir St. John!" she gasped, looking from the golden-haired man leaning against the jamb of the kitchen doorway to the fruit in her hand. In utter dismay at being caught—and by whom!—she knew not which to be ashamed of first: her *deshabille* or her stolen orange. She decided quickly, dropping the orange on the table and grasping her wrapper around her futilely. Her arms were half bare, her feet were entirely so, and her hair was hopelessly escaping the braid into which her maid had so patiently plaited it many hours ago.

To St. John, she looked magnificent.

On his way to the library to find something to distract his thoughts from where they were ever-present these days and his body from the heat he could not escape anywhere in the house, he had heard scuffling in the servants' passage on the other side of the wall. He had wondered with some curiosity who it was that could be about at the dead hour of the night. St. John had followed the sounds downstairs and made his way to the kitchen in search of the night-wanderer, only to be met in the dimly lit room with the enticing vision of a woman's thinly clad backside as she bent over in search of something in his aunt's icebox.

A maid, no doubt, looking for a cool treat when no one could mark her theft. He was intending to disappear quietly down the hall whence he had come when the woman turned suddenly and revealed herself to be the slightly disheveled but altogether delectable-looking Miss Pierce. St. John almost lost his senses.

He retrieved them, however, in time to see the flush steal swiftly over her neck—and what a lovely, slender neck she had—and face. Slowly, casually, he folded his arms across his chest.

"Might there be enough to share, Miss Pierce?" he drawled, a smile lurking at one edge of his mouth as he glanced at the orange.

She looked at him in dismay, horror, and acute embarrassment. Her wide eyes went to the orange sitting solitary on the broad table and then slued almost painfully back to his face.

"Sir—"

He leaned forward slightly, conspiratorially.

"If there are, I shan't tell, if you don't."

Slowly, very slowly, her forehead relaxed and her eyes took on a different light as her lips curved ever so slightly into a tiny grin. Not releasing her hands from the silken wrapper about her, she tilted her head.

"I think perhaps, sir, that there are others in the icebox."

Across the wooden table was scattered enough food and drink to feed a dozen people. The two sitting comfortably on benches on opposite sides of the table were entirely unaware of this.

Sir Pennworthy finished chewing the remains of a piece of crusty bread spread with cheese soft from the night's heat and took a long swallow from the tankard of ale at his right hand. Before Alethea were the remains of an orange, a dish of strawberries, and a rasher of ham that had taken her fancy when they had peeked into the pantry earlier. Having thoroughly abandoned her manners, she was licking her fingers, one by one, of the preserves she had spread on her own slice of bread, an activity that had the man across the table from her nearly breathless with feeling, had she but known it.

St. John finally tore his gaze away from the operation, searching for something else upon which to concentrate until the sensations running through his body faded. They would not. She had seated herself across the table from him, shy of her unconventional state of dress for such a repast. But it had done little good to hide from St. John the beauty of her form, uncorsetted and lithe beneath the soft fabric. He took a deep breath and another drink of ale.

" *'In hoc tu victu saturitatem putas esse,'* Miss Pierce?"

Alethea raised her eyes to his, delight in them. "Indeed, yes, Sir St. John!" she responded with clear contentment. "I am quite satisfied with these scraps we have collected." She swept orange peels together with the edge of her hand and deposited them on the plate that had once contained strawberries. "How excellent you were to be so very sporting about my little midnight raid." Her smile was genuine. For all of the discomfort he was feeling, she seemed to be quite at ease finally. St. John glanced at the mug of ale before her. It was yet half full, but it was a large tankard. He wondered to himself how much ale Miss Pierce was accustomed to drinking at one sitting.

"I am happy for the excuse you have given me to finally explore my aunt's abundant pantry in the middle of the night," he replied promptly, rising to replace the remaining cheese and ham in the larder. He stepped out of the darkness and sat down at the table again. "You know, I believe I have been wanting to do this since I was at least eight years old."

"No!" Alethea said on a chuckle. "How very, very long it took you, sir. You must be terribly principled, or at least very circumspect." She laughed her light laugh, and St. John felt his chest constrict just a tiny bit. "Probably both," she added. "But I am glad you finally relented. This way I shall not be scolded should anyone discover my thefts, as I shall have had your authority upon which to have acted." Her eyes were laughing. But when they looked up at him, awareness sparked and she sobered quickly. "Well," she added more softly, "I expect not."

St. John's lips curved into a slight smile.

"Indeed."

His voice was much sterner than his expression, Alethea thought bemusedly. Then she found herself all of the sudden remembering how he had come upon her and Bertram Fenton in the darkened parlor at the Mowbrays' ball. Suddenly the tingling joy of the adventure she was having dissipated, to be replaced by an uncomfortable tremor of shame. She looked down at the table. His arms rested there, sleeves rolled up to the elbows.

When he had appeared in the doorway, Alethea had noted immediately that he wore almost as little as she relative to the standards from which they were deviating for a meeting between a gentleman and a lady. He had shed coat, waistcoat, and cravat, and his feet were unstockinged, like hers. The shirt he wore was unbuttoned at the neck, his hair dark from damp with the heat of the night on his skin. He looked thoroughly, gorgeously masculine. How had she ever imagined he was not? Of course, she had never seen another gentleman similarly unclothed and so had nothing with which to compare him. But Alethea trusted that he was a unique example, nonetheless.

One of his hands now moved, palm sliding slowly over the smoothed wooden surface of the table. He looked down at it in thought.

"I did say I would not tell, if you do not, Miss Pierce." His tone was light, teasing. She wanted to smile, but could not force herself to.

"Sir, I am truly ashamed of what you have seen of me these past months."

The words were out, could not be taken back. With Herculean effort, Alethea raised her eyes to him. He was looking at her rather oddly, which made it much easier to say what she wished to say.

"You have seen me at my very worst from practically the moment we met. I know it is pointless to deny what a man has seen with his own eyes to be true, but I do wish somehow you could know that I am not as wholly depraved of character as you must believe I am."

St. John's brow rose.

"How low an opinion you must hold of me, Miss Pierce. I should not be here this moment if I thought of you as you have just described."

Alethea stared, wide-eyed, at the man sitting across from her. She felt the tension rush from her as if a gate had been opened, to be replaced by a dullish sort of pain in the region of her chest. She did not know if the feeling was mortification or something quite different.

"Sir, you are generous," she said quietly.

"On the contrary, ma'am. I am not such a fool as to be blind to the power a man has over a woman, even one to whom he is not in any official way attached." He looked at her intently. "You are not to be blamed for his inappropriate actions."

Alethea's eyes flickered, then she sighed quietly.

"I have not been wholly innocent, however, for I cared about him very much—or at least I once thought I did." She looked up over her mug of ale to St. John, and hazel eyes met indigo. Alethea opened her mouth but it was a moment before she could actually make words come forth.

"I am quite aware that this is not an appropriate conversation for us to be having, sir."

"There is nothing whatsoever appropriate about our meeting tonight, madam. I, however, am neither judge nor jury."

She thought then maybe that his eyes sparkled just a little bit, but perhaps it was only the glint from the brass mirrored there. The room hung with the night's heat.

"But," she said, lowering her gaze, "you *have* acted as judge in another matter, have you not?" Alethea felt her cheeks grow warm. Not looking, she missed the expression of discomfort that for an instant traversed the baronet's features.

"I rather like to think," she heard him say finally and she lifted her gaze, "that perhaps you might have done the same if you could have known."

Alethea felt almost physically the intense clarity of the look he turned on her then, and her eyes slowly opened wide. Then she dropped her gaze again quickly. She brushed a strand of dark hair away from her forehead, searching in her muddled thoughts for a response—thoughts muddled more from the ale in her stomach or the man across the table from her, she knew not. His next words, breaking into the silence, surprised her.

" *Tu quidem ita vive, ut nihil tibi committas . . .* '"

" 'Ponder for a long time whether you shall admit a given person to your friendship,' " she translated thoughtfully and finished the phrase, " 'but when you have decided to admit him, welcome him with all your heart and soul.' "

Alethea could feel her face warm again under the baronet's regard, her heart beating heavily within her. He could not know what his championship truly meant to her, or the offer of confidence he made now. Friendship, however, would have to suffice. There were no second chances.

"I thought I cared about Mr. Fenton deeply," she said at length, feeling the interest and understanding from the other side of the table as a tangible thing. She paused for a minute in thought, and ever so slowly the heat and otherworldliness of the night enveloped her. As if of its own will, her heart unburdened itself.

"I was so woefully ignorant. He was not at all what I expected him to be. None of the gentlemen of whom my mother and her friends had spoken so glowingly, so hopefully, were. He flattered my vanity so, and I believed he cared about me, too. But the more I came to learn of him, the more I learned of *gentlemen* and their demands and—and incessant, heedless desires"—she plunged on beyond the scandalous words—"heedless to all things important to *me*, ignoring of *my* feelings and desires, the more I became disgusted with them all. And then finally, in one action, he betrayed my trust in him quite irreparably."

Alethea stared unfocused at the table, biting her lower lip nervously. Finally she cast a glance at the man across from her, and was rewarded with an even look on her companion's face.

"You must forgive my plain speaking, Sir St. John." Her brow was furrowed. "I have been deceived—and so wretchedly so!—by the first man I ever gave my heart to, and sickened by the falseness and rapacity of so many others. I have learned something of a painful lesson, and do not ever wish to have to go through the experience again."

St. John thought that he was maintaining his countenance with admirable equanimity, given that he could barely breathe.

"You have suffered unpardonable indignities."

Was that his voice that had spoken? He hardly knew.

"Indignities?" Her eyes and voice were distant now. "I have been hounded, like a rabbit who knows only fields of clover until the hunt begins." She suddenly laughed and the bitter sound echoed off the shining pots in the candlelit room. Alethea looked hesitatingly up at St. John. "I suppose this is the lot of all women of my class. They search for respect, caring, love, and find presumption in place of what they had expected. All to be tolerated until they give themselves up on the altar of marriage, unless something much worse should befall them first." She fell silent a moment, then uttered blankly, "I do not know why I never understood it before now."

As if coming to herself once more, Alethea shook her head.

"Have I scandalized you finally, sir? I doubt it not."

St. John reached for his tankard and took a long pull of ale. His fingers went to his mouth to wipe it dry. He swallowed again.

"You have not scandalized me, Miss Pierce," he said. "I am not unaware of the existence of the sentiments you express. I have read Madame de Gouges's *Declaration of the Rights of Women.*"

She peered at him intently. Alethea could not believe the baronet quizzed her now, but he seemed to be trying to tell her he understood.

"Then you do not think it odd that a woman would eschew the bonds of marriage, given such a history?"

For a moment he did nothing, and then he shook his head very slightly.

"No."

There was a long silence, neither of them looking at the other, each deep in thought.

"I am perhaps to blame in the larger scheme of things as much as in your private unhappiness, if I may be so bold as to say it, Miss Pierce."

The words were said quietly but with conviction. Alethea looked up at the man across from her and her hazel eyes widened.

It was impossible! She had *entirely* forgotten, in

the midst of her momentary but quite black anger and her need to be understood, that this very man had once proposed marriage to her. How on earth could she have forgotten something that she had spent the *past five months* thinking of almost without ceasing? Alethea's mouth opened in dismay, eyes likewise widening.

"Oh, sir—"

"I have been searching for a wife," he said, interrupting the denial she was poised to voice. He raised dark eyes to hers. She could not read the expression in them. "I believed it was the simplest thing in the world to arrange, and admit that I gave little thought to the lady I chose to bestow my favor upon." Here Alethea thought she spied a hint of color in the gentleman's cheeks, a flicker of his lashes, but in the dim, unstable light she was uncertain. "It was undoubtedly foolish, *I* was foolish, and I am sorry for it." His fingers traced the rim of the mug before him. "How pitiable to simply say I am sorry, when women such as you have borne the arrogance of men such as me."

Alethea reached forward and put her hand on the table between them, wanting to take his but afraid. He looked down at it with a pensive gaze.

"Sir St. John, what led you to seek a wife?" she asked, heart pounding but voice steady enough. "Did your mother or sisters encourage you? Lady Fitzwarren? However much it is customary, it is not the best way to begin married life, I understand, and not a guarantor of profound or even romantic sentiment."

"No, indeed not," St. John replied readily. "But it was not my stepmother's or sisters' will I acted from, nor my aunt's. It was my own. You see, Miss Pierce, I have always wanted to be married, ever since I was but a boy." He shrugged lightly at the confounded expression on the young woman's lovely face. No one could ever believe him, not his sisters, not his valet, not his friends, not even himself sometimes.

"I wished for a bride for many years," he continued, "and believed that when the time came to take one it would not be a difficult thing to devise. In fact, long ago I gave myself a deadline, as it were." He laughed self-deprecatingly. The words were coming out of him with surprisingly little effort. "I determined I would be married by my thirtieth birthday. When that passed, I had learned that perhaps it would take more effort than I had anticipated." Now Alethea was certain his eyes glinted at her, and as she felt her own cheeks redden she was unable to suppress a smile. Had she been the first one he had asked, then? He was remarkable, to laugh at himself and apologize to her despite the discomfort it must surely cause him! "So I spent more time at it. All to no avail. Despite my assiduous efforts I am, alas, yet unbetrothed and not likely to become betrothed in the near future."

His mouth was twisted in a wry grin. Even that expression shaded his face with planes that enhanced its handsomeness yet more. Alethea found it incredible that he had asked and been refused more than once. Certainly, *she* had had reason, but had other women? It was extraordinary, to be sure! She knew at least two dozen girls who would say yes to a proposal of marriage after exchanging a mere "good day" with a man of Sir Pennworthy's wealth and aspect, no matter that he was in Trade—and without even knowing how wonderfully compassionate, honorable, and amusing he was.

Somehow, however, despite all of their confidences of the past minutes, she could not bring herself to voice this conviction. Instead, she stared at his averted profile until he brought his gaze back to hers. A small smile played at the edges of his lips.

" 'Of this one thing make sure against your dying day, let your faults die before you.' " St. John took a visible breath. "Miss Pierce, I tender my apologies to you. Could you, will you, forgive me my impertinence?"

Alethea found her mouth curving into a smile. "If you shall forgive me mine, Sir St. John."

Eighteen

They cleaned up after themselves in companionable silence, Alethea recognizing that she was quite sober after all, and St. John trying not to let his gaze stray too often to the scantily clad beauty moving about the room around him. Then, putting out all of the candles but two, they left the kitchen behind and went quietly down the passageway that led to the main hall. They emerged on silent feet into the high-ceilinged space, and the light of the candles they held seemed to lose itself in the vast entryway. Alethea looked up into the face of the man beside her and turned to him.

"Well, Sir St. John, it has been a delightful evening—morning—to be sure."

He smiled and her knees felt weak.

"The pleasure was all mine, Miss Pierce." His voice was low, almost a whisper.

Neither had thought for many minutes of being discovered together thus by another member of the house party. Now, away from the safety of ale and food and copper pots, they recognized that somehow all was different. The confidences they had shared seemed now to want to scamper away into the safety of the darkness around them. Alethea felt her insides tense as she silently willed the moment not to end, for everything to remain exactly as it was.

"And extraordinary."

St. John heard the words she murmured, as if in his imagination.

"I beg your—"

"Extraordinary, sir. Tonight. It has been a unique experience for me." She was staring up at him with wondering eyes. St. John swallowed hard, hoping against hope she could not read any thoughts in his.

"Of course," she added belatedly.

"You shall sleep well enough now that it is a bit cooler, I hope?" He said with considerable effort, fingers tight around the candleholder.

Alethea had not thought of the heat in hours. She nodded wordlessly and looked at him for another long moment.

"Thank you, sir, again. For everything."

"Thank you, madam." His voice was unmistakably husky.

She turned and made her way to the grand staircase and began to climb it, feeling his gaze on her back as she went. Halfway up, she turned again. He was staring at her, but in the flickering light from his candle she could not read his expression. Then he stepped over to the mantel of the massive hearth and set his candle down on it. As she watched, breath frozen, he walked toward the stair and extended his right hand.

"Dance, madam?"

Alethea gasped. Then she smiled, a hand to her mouth as she felt her heart rise into her throat. Bending, she set her candle down on the step next to her, and then slowly descended the staircase on legs certain to collapse at any moment. When she reached him she put her hand into his and, without warning, he pulled her into his arms.

Alethea had no desire whatsoever to resist. As his mouth came down on hers, her hands stole up around his neck at first tentatively and then more confidently to pull him closer. She felt his hands move across her back, his arms surrounding her, drawing her body against his fully. His mouth was warm, sweet, intoxicating, tasting of ale and heat and desire. Alethea felt his thighs against hers, the heat of his hard body against her breasts as his lips coaxed hers open gently. She responded almost immediately, warming to his kiss as his hand moved to her neck and then the side of her face. He threaded his fingers through her dark, silken hair as his other hand slid down her back to its outward curve, caressing.

Alethea sighed against his lips, and St. John kissed her again, his mouth hungry now as he felt her luxuriant body against his, felt her willingness and passion alive under his hands. He wanted all of her, every bit of body and soul and heart and spirit. Lips parted, her tongue touched his and he heard her groan echo his as his hands moved to touch her more intimately.

He released her quickly if not suddenly, as if coming to his senses. St. John had no such excuse, in reality. He had known each delirious, heart-stopping moment what he was doing, what *they* were doing. Now, looking into her wide, hazy eyes, he felt a desire for her so powerful he could

not catch his breath. Gently disengaging himself
from their embrace, he stepped back from
Alethea, retaining her hand only in a feather
light grasp. He saw her blink, swallow, and part
her reddened lips.

St. John bent over her hand and kissed it, the
touch of his lips sending a frisson of sensation
through Alethea before he released it. She
looked up into inscrutable eyes, dark and
fathomless.

"Thank you," he finally said. Then he moved
over to the mantel, took up his candle, and disappeared down a corridor from the hall.

Left standing alone in the darkness, Alethea
drew her hand up to her trembling lips, moving
the back of her hand across the hot skin of her
cheek. Her fingers strayed to her mouth then,
and when she lowered them her lips remained
open, her eyes staring into the black of the hall.

"Oh."

Alethea never saw sleep that night, or morning, to be accurate. Unable to close her eyes, she
sat in a chair by the window in her room, staring
out at the ever-threatening sky, wondering if *he*
were sleeping. Near dawn, she saw the lightning
and heard the thunder far off. Finally, as the
night turned into gray dawn, the rain began to
pour down in unrelenting sheets on the rose garden and the hill beyond Lady Fitzwarren's house,
bringing a cool, fresh wind in its wake.

She supposed the flowers needed it.

* * *

"Sir St. John is *gone?*"

She was not even aware of the perturbation and surprise in her voice. Alethea sat looking in open, unguarded dismay at her hostess, the pot of tea in her hand entirely forgotten. The countess regarded her from half-lidded eyes, leaning back upon the cushion behind her. Tea spilled over the edge of the cup into the saucer.

"Why, yes, dear. He left this morning before breakfast," Lady Fitzwarren replied smoothly.

"Alethea, darling," Cassandra Ramsay said next to her, "the tea."

Alethea's arm jerked and tea splattered across the table and onto her skirt. She barely felt the heat of it.

"Blast!" she muttered, reaching for a towel, and began to wipe up the liquid trying to run off the table onto the carpet. A parlormaid was instantly at her side, mopping the small spill. She finished and took the soggy towel out of Alethea's hand before moving away. As she dabbed ineffectually at her skirt, Alethea lifted her eyes and surveyed the room confoundedly. Then she looked again to Lady Fitzwarren and noticed that the expression on that lady's face was one more of approval than censure.

"I apologize, Lady Fitzwarren. I cannot think what came over me." She turned to give her friend Cassandra a small, apologetic smile. Lady Bramfield's bright blue eyes revealed nothing— but sympathy?

"Think nothing of it, dear. The kind of thing St. John himself might have done were he here." The countess reached forward for a pastry on the table and picked through several before she found her favorite. Alethea was quite aware now that she should not question the countess any further, but she could not resist.

"How unfortunate that he should have had to depart so soon." She tried to sound casual. "Did he perhaps have work in London to which he needed to return?" She was wearing her heart on her sleeve. She did not care. Countless other girls did it all the time, even for the baronet Pennworthy, were he to ever take notice of them. Alethea felt foolish, but better foolish and informed than foolish and ignorant.

"Oh, he mentioned something about Town, I think, yes. But he travels so very much that it doesn't really signify in the least what he said. You know the boy, not always entirely *articulate*." Lady Fitzwarren affected nonchalance. This affectation at least was obvious enough to Alethea. Her back stiffened. She was being toyed with, and she did not like it a bit.

"I see."

"Alethea, let us go up to your room and I will assist you in changing out of that damp gown." Lady Bramfield set her teacup on the table and stood up. At that moment, Miss Wisterly appeared behind the countess's chair.

"Dear me, Thea, what have you been up to over here? One would think you're becoming almost as scatter-brained as Sir St. Jo—" Belinda's hand went swiftly to her mouth as she moved forward and realized who was sitting hidden from her by the high back of the chair across from her friends. Her eyes widened, but Lady Fitzwarren raised a hand and waved it away.

"I just said the same thing to the dear gel myself, Miss Wisterly. My nephew is the veriest nincompoop at times, of course, however much he never ceases to mean well." She was smiling fondly.

Alethea stood up.

"I cannot understand why everyone constantly picks on the poor man," she said intently. "Forgive me, my lady, Lindy, but I have never seen the baronet act clumsily—a man with his excellent sporting ability could not—and I do not think he merits this or half of the rest of the ridicule he commonly receives." She took a breath. "I am going to my room to change. Excuse me, please."

Alethea turned about and promptly exited the parlor, leaving in her wake the three ladies. Two looked at each other with at first astonished and then comprehending stares. The third settled back comfortably into her chair, chewing on a pastry with what appeared to be extraordinary satisfaction.

Master Seneca was right, on so many accounts. But the one theory that St. John was thinking of at the moment had to do with the length of a day. Unquestionably, because if one day was equal to all days through resemblance, because the very longest space of time possesses no element which cannot be found in a single day, then this day St. John was experiencing was no longer than any other he had ever lived through.

He kept telling himself that as the rain poured down his coat collar and his horse's hooves spattered mud upon his legs and back without intermission. This day was no longer than any other. It did not *seem* to resemble any other day he had ever had, but it certainly must be just the same as all of the others, despite that fact.

Except that today he realized he was both a bigger fool and a bigger scoundrel than he had ever before believed. Perhaps it was true what they all said about him. Only a dim-wit, after all—or a heartless wretch—would have behaved the way he had, not only two nights before but throughout the entire past six months.

And now he was running away. What an honorable fellow he was.

Yet what else was there to do? He was through with it all, through with looking for a wife, through with tendering proposals, through with trying to create for his life something he neither merited nor deserved. Most of all, he was through with being the greatest idiot alive.

He had never, even in his fondest dreams, realized what it was he had been searching for. He had been like a child looking through the window at a chocolate shop, who saw the bright-colored confections, and who admired and desired them without knowing how richly delicious they actually were to taste. St. John had now had his taste, and he wanted much, much more. But the chocolates were not for sale.

Incredible! Incredible what a fool he had been— was! A blind fool, the worst kind. And a selfish, *heedless* one at that. Bertram Fenton may have disappeared for good, but St. John Pennworthy was now conveniently available to take his place, thank you very much. He could not *believe* he had kissed her.

She had felt so warm and delicious in his arms. She had kissed him back. Had she kissed Fenton with such—such *fervor*? Perhaps. She was a passionate woman, clearly. He most certainly did not hold that against her. He was not of the ridiculous opinion held by some gentlemen that ladies did not enjoy intimacy. He knew better. No, Alethea Pierce was a passionate woman who had told him she was sick to her very soul with the arrogance and selfishness of men, and he had gone and *kissed* her as soon as he possibly could have. With nary a by-your-leave.

He deserved this rain. He deserved—although certainly his horses had not—the broken wheel on his carriage yesterday in the drenching downpour. He deserved the hack he had been given this morning out of the inn's stable as a substitute because he was in too much of a hurry to return to London even to await the repairs on his vehicle. He deserved the mud and the wet and the misery of trudging through the wretched weather to reach an empty house and a city that no longer held any charm for him whatsoever because *she* was not there. Had that not been the reason he had left London when he had over a month ago, and not gone home straight away, and instead had wandered aimlessly through the countryside with no direction? Why stay, why leave, why arrive when she was not to be there?

Idiot. St. John knew not what to do now. Perhaps India, perhaps the West Indies. He had plenty of work, plenty to keep him traveling and busy, plenty to do in life now that he was not to have a wife, companionship, a home filled with the one thing he had dreamed of for so many years but had not known how to name. But no matter. Did not someone say that a man alone had the world at his feet? For St. John's courting days were, of a certainty, over. He had fallen in love, and love had made marriage utterly unthinkable.

Nineteen

"You have been reading the same page for a quarter of an hour, Thea. I have been watching you."

Alethea lifted her eyes from the book in her lap and gazed with resignation at her sister. They were sitting in Lady Fitzwarren's library and Octavia was copying maps of the nations of the world out of the countess' historical atlas into a drawing book. Or at least she had been, previously.

"And why have you not been doing something more meritorious with your time, darling Little Sister?" the older girl said flatly.

She would not be baited, nor would she sit around all day explaining herself. If a person had things to think about, she should not constantly be quizzed for being a little pensive. From the comments she had been receiving from Belinda and Cassandra in the past week concerning her solitary walks in the gardens or her breakfasts alone in her room, Alethea was beginning to think her friends had nothing better to do with their time than reflect on how she spent hers. It was really the outside of enough. She would tell them that the next time one of them mentioned it.

Octavia pressed her lips together and shook her head at her sibling.

"You are distracted, and not a little blue-deviled, I think. When he is blue-deviled, Lilly says, Sir St. John goes riding about the countryside. Would it not be grand if we could do the same? Pack a little bag and wander here and there for days on end simply seeing the world?" Octavia's voice was dreamy.

"I am not interested in what Sir St. John does or does not do to relieve tedium, Tavy," she said with a decided lack of patience in her voice. "Now, could you please return to your employment so I can return to mine?" Alethea bent her head to her book again and recommenced pretending to read. Her sister was not to be moved.

"It is not when he is *bored* that he wanders about, but when he is *sad*," she said pointedly, keeping the record straight, "as he did last month when his engagement to Miss Gretehed fell through the boards. Or at least that is what Lilly believes, although he never actually told any of them that he was engaged, or planning on being so. But Lilly said it was nearly a done thing for a while."

"I could not care le—"

"But that was when he wanted a wife, before he changed his mind," Octavia continued blithely, unaware of her sister's interruption. Nor was she aware that her sibling now removed her reading spectacles and stared at her in a rather nonplused manner. "Now he is planning a trip to India, and Lilly says that he has not written a

word to Amelia—their older sister, you know—
about marriage or finding a bride since he has
returned to London, which she says is very unlike
him lately. They all believe he has given up, or
rather, that he has taken a distaste for the idea.
Funny that," she said, brow furrowed as she
traced a rather intricate archipelago, "given that
he was rather *wedded* to the idea before. Ha! I
have made a pun. Papa would be proud."

"Yes, of course he would, Tavy," Alethea murmured, but she barely knew what she said.

"In any case, it seems St. John expects to make
a rather lengthy trip of it this go around, to India, that is. Gone for a year, or two, maybe more,
he says. Lilly and Esther are quite done in by
the idea. He *is* a great gun, but of course you
know that. I envy him the adventures he shall
have . . ."

Alethea's fingers closed the covers of the book
she had not really been reading. She sat straight
up on the chaise. For several minutes as her sister
continued rhapsodizing about India, Alethea
stared at the soft summer rain falling on the
bright green grass beyond the library's window.
Then she set the book down on the chaise, stood
up, and without comment walked out of the
room.

She climbed the stairs not quickly, but neither
slowly, and made her way down the corridor until
she came to the chambers Lord and Lady Bramfield had inhabited for the past weeks. She
knocked. A maid answered the door, and Alethea
entered.

The dressing room was strewn with gowns,
hose, bonnets, shoes, and the paper used to wrap

them all for traveling. Its young, flaxen-haired in-
habitant, sitting in a chair near the partially
opened window, looked up from a frock whose
frayed embroidery she was carefully mending.
She smiled.

"Thea, I was just thinking about you." Cassandra Ramsay rested her hands in her lap as
Alethea came forward and set herself down on
the chaise across from her friend.

"I have been in the library, reading."

Lady Bramfield's eyes bent to her work again.
"You have been doing quite a lot of that lately,
it seems," she commented mildly. Alethea, feeling eons away from where she had been only
minutes earlier, let the comment pass.

"What was it you wished to talk about, Cass?"
she asked instead, fingering the intricate lace on
a flounce of the gown the viscountess was mending.

"Timothy and I were hoping you would join
us in Town for the autumn, as our guest." She
pulled the needle through a fold of cloth and
looked up at Alethea with a smile. "Now that we
will be settling there for an indefinite length of
time, Timothy says he wishes me to have my
friends around me." She smiled sweetly, a slight
flush brightening her cheek. "He is such a kind
man, Thea, so considerate of my feelings and
needs. I would miss you too terribly much if I
were forced to wait for Christmas or even next
Season to see you again, and he knows this without me having to say it."

Alethea reached forward and put her hand on
her friend's wrist for a moment, then released it.

"He is a wonderful man, Cass. I am so glad

you have found him." The sincerity in her own voice surprised even herself.

"Thank you, Thea. I am very gratified you and he get along so well. Do you think you should like to visit with us while your family is in Kent?"

"I should be thrilled to stay in London with you this fall. I shall visit my grandmother in the winter instead, which she always prefers in any case," Alethea said confidently as her friend's happy eyes came up to meet hers. Then she took a breath. "In fact, I was coming to see you about very much the same matter," she said evenly. "Except I was hoping that I might accompany you and Timothy back to Town tomorrow when you leave—at least for a very brief visit, that is. I could return home for the harvest when my parents and Octavia do, of course, and then make my way to you again in September."

Cassandra was now looking at her friend with delicately arched brows, but she said just what Alethea hoped to hear. "Why, certainly you are welcome to come with us tomorrow, Thea. Our home is your home. And you need not return to Kent at all but stay with us through the end of the summer if you wish. I would be so glad to have you with us."

Alethea let out a breath she had not realized she had been holding.

"I suspect—how shall I say?—I believe my business in London will not take me overly long, Cass. And however much I would enjoy remaining with you, I do think you and Timothy should be alone for at least a *little* time before I descend upon you for the autumn." She smiled, then her brow creased and she looked beyond Lady Bramfield's shoulder out the window, distracted by her own thoughts.

"And what—ah—business is it that draws you to London, Alethea? May I ask?" Lady Bramfield's tentative question coaxed her attention back.

"Certainly you may ask, dearest." Alethea took a deep breath and returned a bold gaze to her friend. "I am going there to make a business proposition to a Cit."

St. John was sitting at his desk in his study, ledgers and account books and receipts and miscellaneous papers written in miscellaneous hands spread out before him on the broad surface, when his footman announced a lady visitor. St. John looked up from his work, and his hand went to the back of his taut neck instantly. He flexed his sore shoulders. How long had he not moved from the position he was in? He squinted across the room at the man.

"A lady, Pomley?" he said. "Are you certain? I cannot possibly know one that is in Town at the present time."

The servant nodded his head.

"She is a lady, of a certainty, sir. Not the sort I would call anything else. She has her maid with her," he added significantly.

"Did she say what her name is?" St. John looked down at the ledgers and other items before him with anxious eyes. He did not have time to be entertaining the kind of visitors that a man of his wealth and interests was likely to have at this time of year. Both Pomley and St. John's secretary were accustomed to fielding requests for interviews from enthusiastic inventors, starving artists, and enterprising do-gooders, picking out only the most sincere and least suspicious to bring to their master. St. John was always happy to support a good cause, but Pomley ought to know that this was most assuredly not the time for such an interruption. He was scheduled to set sail for India in less than a week, and he must have his business in order before he departed. St. John did not know exactly when he would be back, but it would not be soon, of that he was certain.

"She did not, sir. She asked to speak with you about an important business matter, but would not say about what or with whose recommendation she comes." The footman lowered his voice. "She is quite—mmm—young, sir. And rather taking, I might add."

"You might?" St. John was amused, but not in the least bit intrigued. Young, attractive females were what got him into this sorry state in the first place. He had less than no interest in meeting yet one more.

"Tell her—"

"Tell her what, Sir St. John?" the young woman said, as she pushed open the door behind Pomley and walked into the room. "That you no longer have time for a woman who does not fall at your feet with gratitude when you so much as look at her?" Miss Alethea Pierce stopped several yards in front of the desk and folded her gloved hands before her. St. John stared.

"That will be all, Pomley."

With what was obviously tremendous reluctance, the footman stepped backward. He drew the door closed in front of him and the maid who stood waiting in the corridor beyond.

Neither Alethea nor St. John saw him go. They were staring at each other, each believing the other's gaze would drop first. Alethea lost the silent battle. Her gaze flickered finally to the piles of papers on St. John's desk, and then to a chair situated in front of the large piece of furniture. She stepped forward and set herself down on the edge of it.

"I have come to speak with you concerning a business matter of great import to both you and me, Sir St. John," she said after a moment when he did not speak. "And I wish you will listen carefully and consider my proposition with the wisdom that I know you must have somewhere inside of your thick head."

"That is not a particularly good way to recommend your petition to me, Miss Pierce. You have clearly never done this before." St. John's heart beat thunderously in his chest, but his tone sounded unremarkable to him, nonetheless.

"I should say not!" Alethea exclaimed. "Although I cannot say the same for you, sir," she added as something of an afterthought. Then she took a breath, both hands clasped on her reticule in her lap, and opened her mouth.

"It has come to my understanding through a reliable source that you are soon to embark for foreign climes. Am I correct?" One soft brow rose in question. St. John swallowed but kept his equilibrium. He nodded.

"You are, madam."

"I have also been privy to the information that you no longer seek a wife. That you have, in fact, quite ceased your search altogether in favor of indefinite bachelorhood, a state coveted by most of the gentlemen of my acquaintance but until recently abhorred by yourself. Do I speak untruths?"

"You do not, Miss Pierce." His response was prompt. St. John feared for the steadiness of his voice, and so kept it brief.

"In short, you have made a rather extreme break from your past in order to set out on a new track," Alethea concluded, eyes almost steady on his face. "Having understood this, Sir St. John, I wondered if you might not, in the interests of allowing me to keep an agreement with myself, change your plans for the future somewhat? As a businessman, I should think you would readily enter into a bargain that benefitted both parties at completion." She seemed to have, for the moment, come to the end of her words; St. John looked what he hoped was encouragingly at her.

"And may I inquire what is the nature of the agreement that you have fashioned with yourself, madam?" he asked, almost blandly. This was quite remarkable.

"Well, sir, I have recently, albeit very recently—on the basis of the actions of someone whom I have previously liked to perceive as an excellent example in many matters—made a change in my life plans as well. I have promised myself that by my twentieth birthday, I should be engaged to be married. The problem is that the day is just around the bend, Friday, to be exact, and I am as yet unbetrothed. Consequently, I thought, Sir St. John, that perhaps if you could be persuaded to reconsider your previous notion of taking a wife, you could oblige me in the small matter of matrimony."

His astonishment could not have been greater had she walked in and announced she was the Queen of England. St. John remained for he did not know how long staring at the young woman sitting across the desk from him. Her hazel eyes were wide, as wide as he had ever seen them, shimmering with unspoken emotion. Her hands were clasped tightly in her lap, and her breathing did not appear at all even from where he sat. Sat? Was he sitting? Impossible! He could not seem to feel his body at all. Well, not most of it, in any case.

St. John cleared his throat. He stood up.

"Miss Pierce," he said, voice lower than he intended. "This is indeed a business proposition which I have never thought to have tendered to me."

The lady came to her feet as well. Her eyes were bright of a sudden—with tears? She was biting one curved, delectable lip.

"And is it a welcome one, or shall I take myself off before I make a cake of myself and cry all over your ledgers and ink bottles here, sir?"

St. John had never moved so quickly in his life. In what was less than an instant, he was around the desk and standing in front of Alethea. With only momentary hesitation, he reached a hand forward and took one of hers gently. His chest felt suffocated.

"Miss Pierce—Alethea, you cannot truly mean this, after what you said to me that night?"

She looked up from their joined hands to his sapphire eyes, as if searching his expression for something.

"I have been so foolish," she said in a shaking voice. "And so lonely waiting for you, St. John Pennworthy, to propose to me again. I thought that I might give it a try this time, seeing that you seemed to have become weary of the job." A smile trembled on her pink lips.

St. John felt an exquisite joy welling up in him, consuming him with unspeakable happiness, and desire. Willing himself control, he raised his hand and touched the soft skin of her cheek. She leaned into his touch, eyes closing slightly.

"This is ex—extraordinary," he murmured wonderingly. "I dare say, I should say yes?" His gaze devoured her face, memorizing every curve, every shade of lash and hair.

Alethea's lips curved.

"You should say yes, and put me out of my misery." She was smiling fully now. "And then you should kiss me, sir, for I have been longing for you to do so for days now, and wish that when you do, you will never, ever stop." Her eyes opened fully, and St. John saw the love in them as clearly as if she had spoken it. He bent his head to hers, her eyelids flickered closed, and her lips parted very slightly. He paused.

"I have just this moment decided that I will not go to India," he whispered just above her mouth. Her eyes opened again. His hands went to her waist and drew her gently against him. St. John could feel her heart pounding rapidly against his chest. His lips moved away from hers a bit, and he looked down at her.

"I believe I shall instead take a wife, now that you suggest it, Miss Pierce. Seems the right thing to do." His voice was light, considering. "You see," he continued, "I believe that if one wishes to importune a lady, that is, if he finds he cannot possibly be satisfied with even standing in the same room with her without wishing to make certain *demands* upon her generosity not to say her person, he had better either take himself off right away—as *some* have been wont to do—or marry her as quickly as possible." Her eyes were warm and sparkling as he watched her, her lips smiling. "After that, of course, he should have to most respectfully ask for her forbearance—"

Alethea raised a hand and batted him ineffectually on one broad shoulder.

"Wretched man!" she cried. "Do not think to turn me away with such paltry humor, because I shan't be swayed." Her eyes narrowed. "You have not answered my proposal yet, Sir St. John. I am of a mind to withdraw it soon. I do not have much experience with business matters, but I am wise enough to know that if a person strings one along in such a fashion, it bodes ill for the outcome of the offer."

Alethea's fingers slid across St. John's shoulders, curled into his hair as she felt his laughter through her body. Then his hands moved to her back, holding her against him more firmly. His gaze moved across her face and Alethea felt her breath catch in her throat at the raw emotion she suddenly saw there.

"Do not withdraw your offer, dearest Alethea,"

he said huskily, mouth close to hers. "What should I do if you did, when all I have been searching for all along is you?"

Their lips met, warm and searching and full of the hunger of each other—a slow, delicious caress of longing and wonder. Finally St. John drew away very slightly, Alethea's mouth following his for a moment before she released him.

"I love you, Alethea." His words were full of wonderment.

"Thank you for waiting for me, St. John," Alethea whispered close to his mouth. "I care not how many refusals you have heard in the past months, except that they have hurt you, and I do not wish you to be hurt. You shall never, ever, my love, hear one again from me."

Several weeks later, on a warm, bright, early autumn morning in London in the Church of St. George, a wedding took place. The event was not out of the ordinary, no larger or smaller than those who were in Town for it expected, a wedding like many others. The guests, however, did note something quite extraordinary, something none of them had ever witnessed before in their lives and which they spoke about for many years afterward. For when it came time to say the vows, the groom, standing beside his bright-eyed yet serene bride, cried.

More Zebra Regency Romances

MILLS & BOON®

Why shop at millsandboon.co.uk?

Each year, thousands of romance readers
find their perfect read at millsandboon.co.uk.
That's because we're passionate about
bringing you the very best romantic fiction.
Here are some of the advantages of
shopping at www.millsandboon.co.uk:

* **Get new books first**—you'll be able to buy
  your favourite books one month before they
  hit the shops

* **Get exclusive discounts**—you'll also be
  able to buy our specially created monthly
  collections, with up to 50% off the RRP

* **Find your favourite authors**—latest news,
  interviews and new releases for all your
  favourite authors and series on our website,
  plus ideas for what to try next

* **Join in**—once you've bought your favourite
  books, don't forget to register with us to rate,
  review and join in the discussions

Visit **www.millsandboon.co.uk**
for all this and more today!